"Stop looking so damned beautiful," Grant said

He continued. "It isn't fair.... I'm a happily to-be-married man. I'm sure this strange effect you have on me will wear off sooner or later, but in the meantime my view is that the best thing is to ignore it. And I would if you'd just stop looking at me like that."

"Like what?" said Rachel.

"As if you wished I'd kiss you."

"But I do wish you'd kiss me," Rachel blurted out. "But I know you're engaged to someone else, so I wasn't about to suggest it."

"All right," said Grant in exasperation. "I can't stand to see a woman cry, and I especially can't stand to see you cry. I'm a teetotaler starting tomorrow. But this is strictly for medicinal purposes." And then his mouth was on hers.

Linda Miles was born in Kenya, spent her childhood in Argentina, Brazil and Peru, and completed her education in England. She is a keen rider, and wrote her first story at the age of ten when laid up with a broken leg after a fall. She considers three months a year acceptable holiday allowance but has never got an employer to see reason, and took up writing romances as a way to have adventures and see the world.

Husband-to-Be
Linda Miles

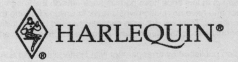

HARLEQUIN®

TORONTO • NEW YORK • LONDON
AMSTERDAM • PARIS • SYDNEY • HAMBURG
STOCKHOLM • ATHENS • TOKYO • MILAN • MADRID
PRAGUE • WARSAW • BUDAPEST • AUCKLAND

ISBN 0-373-17402-0

HUSBAND-TO-BE

First North American Publication 1998.

Copyright © 1997 by Linda Miles.

CHAPTER ONE

A CLEAR February sky was turning a deeper blue, a brilliant orange sun was setting as Rachel Hawkins stepped into the street and left Morrison's Feed & Supply for the last time. Out of another job. And everything had looked so promising too.

She'd run the place perfectly well for two months while Mr Morrison had followed doctor's orders in Marbella. Profits were up, costs down; who could have guessed he'd be so annoyed by a few little changes?

'Perhaps,' he'd said sarcastically, 'you may have noticed the words "feed" and "supply" above the door; you may have noticed the absence of the word "zoo". There is a reason for this, Rachel, and the reason—' a scowl had split the newly tanned face '—is that this is a feed supply business, and not a bally menagerie. I want that lot out by the end of the week.' A dramatic hand had pointed to the back, which was certainly rather livelier than it had been in the days when empty feed sacks had been stacked there. 'And you are going with them.'

Rachel sighed. Looking on the bright side, she'd managed to find homes for all the animals except one. Looking on the dark side, as far as Aunt Harriet was concerned, that probably left one too many. Rachel glanced down dubiously at the box with holes in which she'd put the tiny furry creature. He was quiet and perfectly house-trained, but Aunt Harriet had always refused to have a pet in the house, and something told Rachel that her aunt would not make an exception for William.

Looking on the bright side again, for the first time in years Rachel Hawkins had spent a whole six months not standing thigh-deep in a swamp, providing good, wholesome nourishment for mosquitoes. Any day now the papers would be splashing out in headlines on this new shock to the ecosystem, she thought flippantly. She could see them now: SHOCK! HORROR! PROBE! ACUTE HAWKINS SHORTAGE SPARKS MOSQUITO FAMINE! 'They were dying like flies,' said one horrified observer. Well, it was just too bad, Rachel thought with a grin.

Driscoll had said she'd be bored, but she hadn't been; she'd loved every minute of it. She was still one hundred per cent committed to marrying Driscoll, but Rachel Hawkins was not—repeat *not*—going to be a professional scientist. Of course, going through four jobs in six months maybe didn't give you much time to get bored, she admitted fair-mindedly. But she just knew she'd made the right decision. Sooner or later she'd find the right job. Maybe even a job that let her wear a suit.

A suit. That was what she needed right now, in fact. In the brilliant late afternoon sunshine an adjacent shop window showed only her own reflection dressed for the unseasonably warm weather, haircut to match. Mr Morrison hadn't approved; what would Driscoll think? If only Brian, misfit stable lad and self-taught hair artiste, hadn't decided he was the heir to the flying scissors of Sassoon! His 'practice trim' had left her looking like the scarecrow in *The Wizard of Oz*; she'd had to go to a professional to have it evened up.

'It will have to be very, very short,' the professional had warned ominously.

Rachel had had visions of Julie Andrews in *The Sound of Music*—something short, boyish but very, very chic. She now eyed, doubtfully, the soot-black hair that framed her face, the enormous blue eyes under fly-away brows, the full, almost pouting mouth. Well, it was certainly short.

It would probably look chic, too, if she had, say, a Dior suit to go with it. For some reason, though, she didn't look a bit like the respectable twenty-seven-year-old author of *The Thing From the Swamp, Son of Thing* and *Thing Meets Godzilla*—to use Rachel's personal titles for her research. For some reason she looked like an eighteen-year-old punk. Maybe it was the Doc Martens? The black jeans? Or maybe it was the Spiderman T-shirt. Whatever, Driscoll wouldn't like it.

Rachel sighed. Why was life so complicated? Still, first things first—she must have one last shot at finding a home for William, then find a suit...

And there, down the tiny cobbled street of Blandings Magna, was the suit of her dreams. Half-sleeves, round collar, knee-length skirt, all in a delicious slubbed silk... Of course, it was *on* somebody. It was on a blonde with a spectacular figure—someone who probably looked chic even in a T-shirt. The woman stood by a black Jaguar, perched precariously on absurd stiletto heels—completely unsuitable for the country, of course, but this didn't occur to Rachel. She stared open-mouthed for an instant, then began gravitating down the street towards the Garment of her Dreams. So there *was* such a thing as love at first sight. She'd always wondered.

As she drifted forward, wide-eyed, someone slammed down the boot of the car and a man stood up. An earthquake would not have distracted Rachel from contemplation of the divine object—the way she felt now, she wouldn't have been surprised if the earth had moved—but the man who came into view pulled her up short.

If the woman seemed out of place in a small, drowsy country town, the man was even more so. He had dark blond hair, very brilliant, rather mocking blue eyes in a deeply tanned face, and a mouth that looked as though it

could be hard, though at the moment it was quirking with
amusement. He was conventionally dressed in a dark suit,
but everything about him said that here was someone who
went after what he wanted; if convention was between him
and it, convention had better get out of his way.

He was certainly very good-looking, but it was not this
that made Rachel stare. Something about him was oddly
familiar—hadn't she seen those deep blue eyes before?

'Any luck, Grant?' the woman asked in a husky drawl.
And suddenly Rachel placed him. It was Grant Mallett, of
course—but what was *he* doing in a suit and tie? Rachel's
idea of keeping up with current events was to read *Vogue*
and *Scientific American*, but even she had heard of Grant
Mallett.

He'd been labelled everything from eco-warrior to rab-
ble-rouser, but Rachel wasn't fooled; this was a man who
landed in trouble the way some men just naturally ended
up in the nearest bar. If a tribe was being pushed out of its
territory by loggers in the heart of the Amazonian rain-
forest, you could bet Grant Mallett had just happened to
canoe a couple of hundred miles up an obscure tributary to
turn up in the middle of the fracas. If poachers went after
ivory in a Kenyan game reserve, it would just naturally be
on the night when Grant Mallett had gone out on safari and
accidentally got left behind.

He was *persona non grata* in eight separate countries,
including his own; a man who'd been cursed in thirty or
forty languages by officials who were 'just doing their job';
naturally the British Press adored him. And he was definitely—but definitely—not Rachel's type.

Rachel could get in quite enough trouble on her own
account without someone like Mr Six Adventures Before
Breakfast here. Go around with someone like that and you
wouldn't just find yourself standing in a swamp all your
life—you'd find that the swamp was infested with piranhas.
Thank goodness she was engaged to Driscoll—sensible, ma-

ture, reliable Driscoll. But what in heaven's name could this lightning-rod in human form be doing in Blandings Magna? And what was the lovely blonde doing with him? It was, in Rachel's opinion, an unnecessary risk to a perfectly good suit.

'Sorry, Olivia, we must have left it back at the house,' said Mr Mallett. Something in his voice suggested that the 'we' was for politeness' sake.

Olivia shrugged. 'Oh, it doesn't matter, darling. Let's just have a quick look in this antique shop before it closes, shall we? They might have something that would do for the private part of the house.'

Most of the residents of the village had acquired a pet from Morrison's in the last month or so. Rachel now realised suddenly, joyfully, that one had not. Joyce, in the antique shop, was new to the district; she had a soft spot for William; probably she'd be only too pleased to have him for her very own.

She followed the couple into Blandings Magna Antiques. 'It's absolutely thrilling that you've decided to go through with it,' said the woman, in a bored, drawling voice strangely at odds with her enthusiastic words. In anyone else Rachel might have thought it affected, but in her eyes the owner of The Suit could do no wrong. *That* was what she wanted to be like. Suave. Sophisticated. Someone who didn't even *own* a pair of thigh-high rubber boots, never mind wear them. 'Daddy says you might even get a knighthood, did I tell you?'

'Oh. Hell. That is, terrific—but there's many a slip,' Mallett said hopefully. 'It may yet come to grief. I thought the countryside had high unemployment, but I can't even find a secretary...'

He joined her to look at a cherrywood dresser.

Rachel stopped, starry-eyed, on the threshold. That was what she'd be! She'd be a secretary! She saw, in an instant, a vision of herself in preposterous heels and a sophisticated suit, seated at a desk; air-conditioning would cool her in the summer, central heating warm her in winter. A coffee-maker in a beautifully appointed kitchenette would dispense freshly made coffee from freshly ground beans, while somebody who *wanted* an academic career stood in swamps and toughed it out with a battered Thermos.

While she stood at the door revolving visions of a wall-to-wall-carpeted, mosquito-free environment, the couple made its way slowly about the room, Olivia commenting on each item of furniture in exhaustive detail. Sometimes the flow was broken by a comment shot to Joyce—usually a disparaging remark about the price. Or sometimes a question was put to Mallett—but Mallett, who had always been decisive, indeed obdurate to the point of insanity on the question of, say, conditions in a refugee camp, now only shrugged and deferred to the views of his companion.

'Whatever you think,' was his constant reply. 'I don't know much about it; it looks all right to me; the money's not a problem if you want it.'

'But Grant,' Olivia protested at last, 'it's not just for me, it's for us. Surely you must have some opinion.'

Even Rachel, preoccupied with the double problems of a home for William and her future career as the perfect secretary, could not repress a certain interest in this development. Mallett had replied politely to all the questions put to him, but it was obvious enough that he had been fighting down colossal boredom with the subject. He certainly seemed the last person in the world to make the beautifully finished creature beside him happy. Were they about to discover their mistake? Would he feel trapped? The couple had stopped by a sideboard with a mirror set in the back; Rachel got a clear view of the rueful, humorous look in the blue eyes—no hint of regret there.

'Olivia, my opinion is that the place will look a lot better if you follow your instincts instead of listening to someone who thinks a tent with a folding chair is overfurnished. I'm pretty certain the science park will work in that location; I'm sure the house will work well for conferences, and I'm sure we can be comfortable in it. I'm glad to be settling down at last, but I haven't got out of the habit of expecting to fit my living quarters in a rucksack. I keep thinking you'd be lucky to get that thing a mile in a jungle, which I admit is ridiculous when it will never have to leave the dining room—just give me a while to get used to the idea of having a dining room, will you?'

Olivia shook her head. 'Where would you be without me?' she asked.

'I can't imagine.' He smiled down at her, shaking his head.

Even Rachel, who knew her type—and Grant Mallett wasn't it—had to admit that the smile was pretty devastating. But Olivia seemed oddly immune; she raised one perfectly groomed eyebrow, and turned her attention again to the sideboard.

Rachel was about to return to her daydream when she was interrupted by Joyce, a woman with pepper-and-salt hair and the rather sardonic look of someone who has spent a lot of time in the antique trade. She'd been doing something or other with paperwork, in between replies to Olivia, just to take the pressure off the visitors; now a chat with Rachel looked just as good a way to put potential clients at ease. 'Rachel!' she exclaimed with pleasure. Her eyes fell to the box. 'Don't tell me—it's not William?' Joyce had heard all about Mr Morrison's lack of enthusiasm for innovations at the Feed and Supply.

''Fraid so,' said Rachel, clearing her head of a scene in which she opened the morning post with an enamelled letter opener elegantly held in a perfectly manicured hand. 'The thing is that Basil and Stephen and Christopher all had such striking colouring that they went straight away, whereas poor old William…'

Joyce shook her head sympathetically. 'So you're keeping him yourself?'

'Well...'

'Let's have a look.' Joyce took the box, slid back the top, and looked fondly down. 'Isn't he a lamb?' she said dotingly. William had just eaten and was sitting drowsily in one corner, but this was nothing to the eye of love.

'I was actually wondering whether you wouldn't like to have him?' said Rachel, recognising her cue. But the reply was one she'd heard dozens of times before.

'I'd *love* to,' Joyce said regretfully. 'But I really don't think Jack would stand for it. You know what men are like. And it would simply wreak havoc if I kept him in the shop.'

Rachel sighed. She could hardly complain. She did know what men were like. Hadn't she asked Driscoll? And hadn't Driscoll said no?

She realised, suddenly, that The Suit was coming towards them. Mallett—who needed a secretary, and didn't realize that one was standing in that very room—was examining a rather moth-eaten tapestry on the far wall.

'I'm interested in the dining-room chairs,' said Olivia. 'Isn't there some sort of reduction for the set?'

Rachel tactfully withdrew. Time to approach her new employer.

'Excuse me...' she began.

'Yes?' He turned to look down her; one preposterous eyebrow shot up at the T-shirt; a smile lurked on his mouth. He wasn't her type, of course, but she had to admit that he was an eyeful.

'I was wondering—'

And suddenly, with dreadful clarity, she heard a sentence from across the room.

'What's in the box? Is it a kitten?'

Rachel turned just in time to see Olivia take the box from Joyce and hold it up playfully. Suddenly, chillingly, it occurred to her that Olivia might be the kind of woman who thought it was engaging to take a small, fluffy animal and put it on her shoulder or in her hair. Something in the charming way she had just tossed back her blonde hair suggested the worst.

Olivia had stopped trying to see through the tiny holes; she was now tugging at the lid of the box.

'Please leave him alone,' said Rachel hastily.

'Don't be silly. I love animals,' Olivia said sharply. The lid came suddenly off the box.

With almost comical haste Olivia's head shot back as she recoiled instinctively with an exclamation of disgust. One of the preposterous heels skidded on the polished floor, then caught in a knot in the wood; the hand holding the box jerked, and the hapless William shot into the air, then fell to cling precariously to the lovely suit.

'A-a-agh!' A terrible shriek split the air. Olivia was brushing frantically downwards with the box.

'Oh, do be careful!' cried Rachel, rushing forward. But before she had come to the rescue the woman had at last knocked William to the ground. He slid smartly across the waxed boards, straight past Rachel, to bounce back against the wall at Mallett's feet. He lay there for a moment or two, dazed but apparently uninjured, then began to hop clumsily away.

'Kill it, Grant!' shouted Olivia. 'Kill it! Kill it!'

And to Rachel's horror Mallett automatically turned, looked round for some sort of weapon, found none, and raised a foot.

There was only one thing to be done.

Rachel hurled herself at him in a tackle.

In the ordinary way, of course, there was no way that Rachel could have brought down a man a good six inches taller and fifty pounds or so heavier than herself; but he was off balance, one leg raised, the better to stomp on William. They toppled to the ground with a momentum that made the floor shake.

There was a moment's dead silence.

Out of the corner of her eye Rachel saw Joyce take back the box and scoop William into it.

One worry taken care of. Well, at least she had his attention.

'I understand you're looking for a secretary,' said Rachel.

The man beneath her, who seemed to be a mass of solid muscle, shifted slightly, so that Rachel slid from his muscular back to the floor. It occurred to her, belatedly, that it might not have been the best moment to bring up possible employment.

In a sudden, swift movement, he sat up and fixed her with an impossibly blue gaze. 'A simple secretary by day... What's your name?'

'Rachel.'

'A simple secretary by day, the scourge of criminals by night, Rachel, the Girl Spider, was to outward appearances like any other girl,' he told her solemnly. 'Little did her unsuspecting colleagues suspect that that demure exterior concealed a relentless crusader against all tramplers of the innocent and defenceless... I think I was thinking of someone with more conventional qualifications. Ever thought of working as a bodyguard?'

He wasn't her type, but Rachel couldn't help but be warmed by the laughter in the blue eyes. He was laughing at her, but he could have taken it worse. And he hadn't said no—at least, he hadn't said anything that she had to take as no for an answer.

'I'd rather be a secretary,' she said eagerly. 'And I've got lots of qualifications. I'm sorry I jumped on you, but I was afraid you'd kill William.'

'Oh, for God's sake.' The scornful voice was Olivia's. 'What the blazes were you doing carrying something like that around in a box? I could have been killed!'

Rachel jumped to her feet, followed, with lazy grace, by

her victim. 'No, you couldn't,' she said crossly. Not even from The Glorious Suit would she take that kind of nonsense.

'He's a *Mexican* tarantula,' she explained patiently. 'So even if he did bite you it wouldn't be dangerous, and he wasn't *going* to bite you because he'd just been fed and was sleepy. *You* might have killed *him*, dropping him so carelessly. They're very fragile, you know. Their bodies are just a brittle shell, so if you drop one it can crack and die.'

Rachel scowled. 'I think it's a bit much to kill an innocent spider that wasn't doing anyone any harm,' she added irritably. 'You wouldn't kill a dog for being in the same room with you, even if it *could* bite. Why should William be any different?'

Olivia came to take Mallett's arm. He put it round her, and she nestled inside—rather implausibly, Rachel thought. 'That's nonsense,' she said faintly. 'I was terrified. Thank God you were here, Grant.'

This touching scene was interrupted by Joyce, who said practically, 'But Rachel's perfectly right, you know. He's not at all aggressive—a perfect lamb, really.' By way of demonstration she took William carefully from the box and placed him coolly on the flat of her hand.

Even now—jobless, and with a home still to find for William—Rachel could not help watching with a thrill of pride.

She'd trained as a zoologist, then specialised for years in ecology. When she'd tried to leave the field the feed and supply shop hadn't been her first, or her second, or even her fifth choice job. When Mr Morrison had had to go to Spain unexpectedly, however, she'd been staying with her aunt and had agreed to help out.

In the owner's absence Rachel had begun a sideline dealing in unwanted pets—creatures people had impulsively acquired and lost interest in, and which might otherwise have been abandoned. These had included several tarantulas, whose owners had got bored, and gradually Rachel had built up a small insect zoo.

She'd discovered that nine out of ten people seemed to dislike spiders in degrees ranging from mild distaste to severe phobia—and this in a country where all spiders were harmless and only a few were even capable of piercing human skin.

By her third week in the shop Rachel had been giving classes to people who wanted to overcome this, on the principle that anyone who could get used to a tarantula was unlikely to be worried by the odd spider in the bath. She'd even taken William to classes in local schools. The result was that the population of Blandings Magna was probably the freest of prejudice against spiders of any in the kingdom.

Joyce had been so nervous of spiders that she'd sworn it was wrecking her marriage—she'd had Jack inspect every room before she went in, to make sure the coast was clear, had been paralysed with fear if a spider appeared in the bath, had hardly been able to go into the cobwebby attics and cellars where some of the best antiques turned up. And now look at her! No, come what might, Rachel knew she'd used her time well.

Olivia did not reply. She was still cowering against Mallett's muscular chest. Rachel was capable of being endlessly patient with people with genuine phobias, but she had spent too much time with them not to know the difference between the real thing and a fake. The woman's original shock had been real, but now she seemed to be quite coolly turning it to her own purposes.

'It's all right, darling.' Mallett stroked the blonde hair, his voice gentle; whatever her scepticism about Olivia, Rachel gave him full marks for his treatment of someone he thought genuinely terrified. 'You probably weren't in any danger, but I know they can be horrible to look at.' He glanced at Joyce. 'We take your point, but I think it might be better if you put him back in the box.'

It seemed to Rachel that the conversation was drifting away from the subject of real importance. 'I'd be a wonderful secretary,' she told him. 'You just said you couldn't find one. Why couldn't I be yours?'

Olivia burst into scornful laughter.

'I'm afraid I need someone familiar with scientific terminology,' Mallett said tactfully. 'It goes beyond the ordinary secretarial skills.'

'But I am familiar with scientific technology. I—I studied biology at school,' said Rachel. Perfectly true, as far as it went. If she went any further and told him about all her degrees and research papers she knew what would happen: she'd find herself standing thigh-deep in a swamp before you could say Jack Robinson.

'He also needs someone with a rather different style of presentation,' Olivia said sarcastically.

This was a subject dear to Rachel's heart. 'Well, naturally I wouldn't dress like this for the office,' she said. 'I'd wear a suit. One like yours would be just right.'

Olivia's eyes widened, and then she gave a rather malicious smile. 'I'm sure you're right,' she drawled. 'Karl is such a genius. I'll give you the number of his showroom; maybe you can drop in next time you're in Paris.'

Rachel flushed as the implication of this sank in. 'Well—maybe I'd have to settle for a cheap imitation,' she said gallantly.

'Could be,' Olivia said coolly. She glanced at Joyce. 'Well, thanks for showing us round.' Her eyes fell pointedly to the box in which William was once again immured. 'I don't think we'll be needing those chairs, but I'll let you know. Come on, Grant.'

Mallett gave Rachel a wink. 'Chin up,' he said. 'I'm sure the right job will come along.'

The door closed behind them with a tinkle.

'I'm awfully sorry; I lost you a sale, didn't I?' said Rachel.

Joyce shrugged. 'Well, probably, but they're lovely chairs—I'd hate to think of them wasted on *her*. The thing is, though, what on earth is Driscoll going to say?'

CHAPTER TWO

RACHEL knew what Driscoll was going to say. He was going to say she should apply for another research grant, and stand full-time in a swamp, or for a lectureship, and just stand in swamps doing fieldwork in the summer. He was going to say that if she didn't want an academic career there was plenty of work in the private sector. He was going to bring up again his old idea of setting up an ecological consultancy together as part of an environmental assessment team.

Rachel knew she should be grateful. After all, you heard such terrible stories about men who didn't like women to be their intellectual equals. Driscoll, to do him credit, took her career as seriously as he took his own.

He'd been thrilled by the prizes she'd won as an undergraduate, thrilled by the industry sponsorship she'd won for her doctoral research, thrilled by the awards her work had won. He'd collaborated with her lots of times when she'd been asked to help with environmental assessments relating to her area of expertise. He'd always insisted that she should be as dedicated and single-minded about her work as he was about his own, constantly developing a track record of publications, papers at conferences and consultancies.

Probably that single-mindedness was what she admired most about him. Driscoll was so mature about everything. He didn't seem to mind the horrible boredom you had to put up with if you wanted to climb the academic ladder, or wanted to carve out a niche for yourself as a consultant. He just accepted mind-numbing specialisation as the price you had to pay for being a professional, whereas somehow Rachel never had got used to it.

She'd enjoyed her first research project, as an undergraduate, when she'd done a study of a bed of reeds and its inhabitants. Then it had won a prize, and then it had turned out that she was supposed to go on doing specialised population studies for the rest of her life, sometimes in a mangrove swamp, sometimes in the pampas, but always in a little area of research that she was supposed to make her own. All the other things she'd loved about zoology would be things of the past, unless she was lucky enough to teach a course on one some day. The main business of her life would be an expert on standing in swamps and counting what turned up there.

Rachel stared unseeingly down at the carrier bag in which William's box was now concealed. Driscoll just didn't seem to realise that she wasn't cut out for a scientific career the way he was. She would be perfectly happy to go with him to whichever university gave him a permanent job—just as soon as he *got* a permanent job. Then she would find something interesting to do, and leave Meals on Wheels for Mosquitoes behind her.

Meanwhile she had to convince him that there was something else she was really cut out for, or he'd start nagging her to publish some more research, or, worse, actually do some more research. Confound Grant Mallett. He needed a secretary. She'd be perfect for the job. Why couldn't he see that?

Still mulling over this problem, she sneaked into her aunt's house by the back door, tiptoed upstairs to her room and put William's box in the closet. Naturally she couldn't keep him without consulting her aunt, but the subject was a delicate one; she just had to find the right moment.

That this was not the right moment was clear as soon as

she'd traced her aunt to the kitchen. 'Men!' cried Aunt Harriet in disgust, chopping vegetables amid chaos. 'Your uncle!' she added darkly, ferociously dicing an onion. 'Would you believe that he could decide to bring someone home for dinner on a Friday night, with*out* warning, when he knows I do my weekly shopping on Saturday? What, I ask him, am I supposed to feed this guest? Dog food *au gratin*? "Oh, anything will do," is the helpful reply. "He's used to roughing it!" *Roughing it*!' The blade smacked solidly down on the chopping-block.

Rachel devoted herself to putting together a salad. Perhaps this was not *quite* the time to mention another unexpected guest.

'Who is it?' she asked.

'How should I know?' Aunt Harriet asked belligerently. 'I just cook here.' She began morosely sautéing the onion in a skillet. 'Some man who wants your uncle to do some renovations,' she added dourly.

An hour later a respectable supper was on its way to being ready. Aunt Harriet seemed to want to brood over the finishing touches in solitude; Rachel retired to the front room to leaf through the fashion pages.

'This spring, keep it simple,' was the reassuring advice. 'No fuss, no frills; perfect cut says it all. The shift, in bright white or fire-engine red, with a pair of strappy sandals...'

Rachel glanced gloomily down at her faded jeans, then back at the picture, where the model sat on a bar stool in a dazzling white shift—a snip at three hundred and fifty pounds. According to her magazine, you could wear it anywhere, but Rachel knew you couldn't. That was what she liked about it. No one in her right mind would pay that kind of money for a dress, slip on a pair of strappy sandals and wade out into a stream to stain its hem with phytoplankton. It was a dress that demanded respect; wear it and no one would expect you to do anything more energetic than shop for another pair of strappy sandals.

Rachel was distracted from these wistful thoughts by the sound of two sets of footsteps approaching down the front walk. 'Such a shame,' said a familiar voice. 'I'm afraid she wasn't feeling well.'

Rachel sat up as if shot. If only she'd known! Another chance at the perfect job, and here she was, still in her Spiderman T-shirt...

But the door to the sitting room had opened. 'Rachel, Mr Mallett will be staying to dinner,' Uncle Walter explained. 'Mallett, my niece, Rachel.'

Mallett stopped for an instant in the door, then came forward, his face alight with laughter. 'We met earlier this afternoon,' he said. 'This is an unexpected pleasure.' Polite, conventional words—but the brilliant blue eyes really did seem to be sparkling with delight. It occurred to Rachel that if she'd gone by his reputation she'd have expected someone hardbitten, cynical, world-weary. People had actually tried to *kill* him—yet he seemed to regard life as something arranged for his own amusement.

'Isn't that nice?' said Uncle Walter. 'Well, you'll just have to entertain each other—Rachel's fiancé can't be here either. I'll just see if I can appease your aunt, dear—see if Mr Mallett would like a drink.'

'Would you like a drink?' asked Rachel politely.

'Scotch and water. I didn't know you were engaged,' said Mallett, dropping into a chair and crossing impossibly long legs in front of him.

'We've only just met,' Rachel pointed out.

'True enough. Who's the lucky man?'

'There's a picture of him,' said Rachel, handing him the drink.

Mallett took it. He glanced at the picture, which showed Driscoll, with black-rimmed glasses and black hair neatly parted, in a graduation photo, and burst out laughing. 'You're not marrying him?' he exclaimed.

'Of course I am.' Rachel glared at him.

'Is it a bird? Is it a plane? No, it's mild-mannered Clark Kent. You can't be serious.'

'Driscoll is a first-rate researcher,' said Rachel. 'Not that it's any business of yours. I applied for a job as your secretary; I did not ask for your advice on affairs of the heart.'

Mallett raised a preposterous eyebrow; he still seemed to regard the whole thing as a joke. 'You seem to have the most extraordinary ideas of how to run your life,' he commented. 'I've only known you a couple of hours and even I can see this Driscoll isn't up to your weight. And, as if that isn't enough, you have the peculiar idea that you want to be a secretary. Can't you find an opening as a lion-tamer?'

'If I weren't too polite,' countered Rachel, 'I might ask why you were planning to spend the rest of your life with a clothes-horse.'

He grinned. 'But naturally you're too polite. There's a lot more to Olivia than meets the eye. Anyway, you're just going by my reputation, which is highly exaggerated.' The happy-go-lucky face was suddenly, unexpectedly serious. 'But you're right, of course—it is a departure. It's time I settled down.'

He took a sip of his drink, then gave her a rueful grin. 'The thing is, I've never settled to anything—something always comes up. I was going to be a scientist, you know— went off to Brazil to do an MA on sugar cane and soil erosion, suddenly this land-rights dispute blew up. Well, naturally I couldn't sit on the sidelines. Finally I got kicked out of the country.

'So my supervisor came up with another topic, and I went off to Malaysia—same result. Finally he got fed up with pretending I was going to finish a thesis. One thing led to another—I've made a fair amount of money over the years, and got a few people out of hot water, but you can't go on that way indefinitely. That's why this science park will be so great. We can give facilities to a lot of innovative inventors, see if they can't come up with solutions to some serious problems.'

'Hmm,' said Rachel.

Mallett shook his head. 'The thing I can't get over is the way some people stay out of trouble,' he said. 'Everybody's heard of me, but what does it all add up to? The man I really admire is someone you've probably never heard of— R. K. V. Hawkins. Amazing guy. No heroics—just an incredible record of solid research that no ecologically respectable company can afford to ignore.' He finished his whisky and set it down. 'Funny we never ran into each other, really—we've been in a lot of the same places.'

Rachel Katherine Victoria Hawkins opened her mouth and shut it again. She knew what would happen. She would tell Grant Mallett that he'd met the man of his dreams— and, next thing she knew, it would turn out he had a swamp he wanted her to go and stand in because the mosquitoes were looking run down.

'I'm afraid I haven't heard of him,' she said truthfully.

Before Mallett could say any more about his hero, Aunt Harriet and Uncle Walter came in to announce dinner. The small group quickly filed into the dining room, and the discussion rapidly moved to the subject of the innovations to be introduced at the hall.

Rachel listened with gathering interest. The science park sounded a wonderful idea—she found herself positively drooling at some of the facilities Mallett wanted to provide. And the maddening thing was that she thought she probably would be perfect to coordinate and liaise at this end while Mallett travelled back and forth to London.

Meanwhile, Uncle Walter brought the conversation round to Mallett's adventures. For the second time that day, Rachel had to give credit to Mallett for surprising niceness. You'd have thought he had nothing better to do in the world than repeat, for probably the five-hundredth time, a lot of stories for a middle-aged man of no influence or importance.

Uncle Walter and Aunt Harriet punctuated the stories with admiring exclamations of, 'You don't say!' and 'Think of that!' Even Rachel was interested to hear some of the details that hadn't made it to the Press—though naturally she was glad *she* wasn't involved with the kind of man who let this kind of thing interfere with his research. Thank goodness Driscoll was more sensible.

'Of course, Rachel has had quite an eventful career,' began Uncle Walter. For a horrible moment Rachel expected her secret to be revealed. But Mallet came to her rescue.

'I'll bet she has!' he exclaimed. 'She's quite a character, isn't she?' He grinned. 'It's not every girl, after all, that carries around a genuine Mexican tarantula as a companion. I met William this afternoon.'

There was a small silence.

'William?' said Aunt Harriet ominously.

'Er…' said Rachel.

'I suppose,' said Aunt Harriet, 'that you were delivering him to a client?'

'Er…' said Rachel. 'Not *exactly*.'

'Do you mean to say,' said Aunt Harriet, 'that you have brought one of those frightful creatures into *my house*?'

'I was going to ask you—' began Rachel.

'No,' said Aunt Harriet. 'I am not having one of those things under my roof.'

'But it's just till I find him a home,' Rachel said pathetically.

'Certainly not,' said Aunt Harriet. 'Driscoll wouldn't like it. I can't imagine what he'll say when he finds out—'

And at this there was an unexpected interruption. 'Well, if Driscoll wouldn't like it it's obviously out of the question,' said Mallett, all wide-eyed innocence. 'Tell you what, Rachel—you can keep him over at Arrowmead.'

'How do I know I can trust you to look after him?' asked Rachel.

'Oh, you'd have to come and feed him,' he said cheerfully. 'Unless, of course, you think Driscoll would object.'

Rachel ground her teeth. 'Of course he wouldn't object!' she exclaimed. Well, not once she'd explained, anyway. She paused, then added, 'You know, if I'm going over there anyway, I might just as well be your secretary.'

'A secretary!' exclaimed Aunt Harriet, shocked. 'Rachel, I don't think Driscoll would like that at all!'

And now a look of pure devilry came into the brilliant blue eyes. 'Do you really think so?' said Grant Mallett. 'Because I'm beginning to think Rachel is just the girl for the job!'

once was. We ardied away... on can leave him at your house so he won't feel lonely.

When do you want me to start work?' asked Rachel.

Well, if you could have... Amanda, that would be good...

No, I couldn't be away.

Good. I'll see... tomorrow... when I've sorted out...

And again... to pick her up... As you... seem to see...

...

sure they'll have time to explain.

Here's one of the...

CHAPTER THREE

'How could you?' Rachel said accusingly. She stood by the Jaguar outside the house, William's box in her hand, and glared at William's future host, her new employer.

'How could I what?' Grant asked innocently. 'Have seconds of dessert? Separate you from your favourite pet?'

'You know perfectly well what I mean,' said Rachel. 'How dare you talk that way about Driscoll? You don't even know him!'

'I didn't say a word!' he protested. The brilliant eyes danced. 'It was your *aunt* who thought he wouldn't like William, remember? And how could I possibly disagree? As you say, I don't even know him.'

'So why did you give me the job just to annoy him?'

'I think you're imagining things,' said Grant. 'You kept telling me how good you'd be, and I *do* need someone down here fast. You convinced me you'd be a good thing. Of course, I have to admit that a man who'd even object to your working as a secretary sounds pretty Victorian. This is the twentieth century, after all, and women have just as much right as men to economic independence—but that's for the two of you to discuss. I'm a complete outsider. It's hardly for me to express an opinion, is it?'

'No, it isn't,' Rachel agreed emphatically, but she gave up the argument as a bad job. 'Do be careful with William, won't you?' She handed him the box.

'I'll make sure no one bothers him,' he assured her. 'And

once you've started work you can keep him in your office, so he won't feel lonely.'

'When do you want me to start work?' asked Rachel.

'Well, if you could manage Monday that would be great, but I realise it's short notice—'

'No, Monday's fine.'

'Good.' There was a short pause in which he seemed, uncharacteristically, at a loss for words. At length he set the box on top of the car and dug into a pocket. 'Look, I hope you won't be offended, but I'm still trying to raise some funding for this, so presentation actually does matter. I realise you weren't planning to dress like this for the office, but you may still find an office job five days a week puts an unexpected strain on your wardrobe. Why don't you go into town tomorrow and see if you can't find a use for this? I don't suppose they run to Paris couture, but I'm sure they'll have something suitable.'

He took out a thick sheaf of banknotes and pressed them into Rachel's hand.

'Good, then that's settled,' he said hastily, snatched William's box off the car, opened the door, and slid into the driver's seat before Rachel could murmur a word of protest. The powerful motor roared into life—and the car disappeared down the street while Rachel discovered that she'd just had seven hundred pounds, in *cash*, thrust into her hand.

Rachel had qualms, at first, about actually spending the money she'd been given—but then a terrible, irresistible thought occurred to her. If she bought clothes with it she would have an ironclad reason why she couldn't possibly give up the job—something Driscoll would otherwise be sure to insist on as soon as he heard of it.

She went into Canterbury and spent a day ecstatically buying separates. Previously, separates in Rachel's wardrobe had consisted of T-shirts and jeans; now she acquired skirts in linen and silk, jackets, blouses, even a couple of waistcoats.

Maybe she didn't look like Julie Andrews, she thought, admiring herself in a fitting-room mirror, but there was no doubt about it—the new clothes did make her look less like the drummer in a rock band and more like some sophisticated icon of the screen. It was just like Eliza being transformed into Miss Eliza Doolittle in *My Fair Lady*, she decided. 'How kind of you to let me come,' she said to her reflection, trying to look like Audrey Hepburn. 'The rain in Spain falls mainly in the plain.'

Driscoll never seemed to notice how Rachel looked: even on very grand occasions, when she set out to dazzle, the only thing that ever interested him was who'd got tenure. She'd come to take it for granted. That was just the way men were. The reaction of her new employer came as something of a surprise.

'*Wow,*' said Grant, the brilliant blue eyes seeming to widen to twice their normal size, and to blaze at about fifty times their normal intensity. Rachel had been escorted by some kind of man-of-all-work down long, dusty halls, through rooms swathed in sheets, to emerge at last at a small, chaotic office at the back of the house. Grant was leafing through stacks of brochures, drinking coffee out of a plastic cup. He'd looked up and clutched ostentatiously at the table for support.

'Catch me if I fall,' he told her. 'I don't think I can stand the shock. Did I say wow? I always think understatement is so much more effective, don't you?' He gave a wolf-whistle, which was probably his idea of something subtle and understated.

'Let me get a good look at you,' he added, putting down the coffee and walking around her to get the full impact of the very pale pink suit, its skirt as short as was consistent with good business practice, and high-heeled pink slingbacks. Rachel had made her face up—the kind of thing that fieldwork did not leave much scope for—with very pale foundation and lipstick, and just the faintest touch of charcoal eyeshadow and black mascara on her lashes; she'd thought the extra formality of the look was needed to counterbalance the rather shocking haircut. Her efforts seemed to have paid off.

'Just promise me one thing,' Grant said very seriously as he came round to the front again.

'What's that?' Rachel asked suspiciously.

'Promise me you will never, ever again wear jeans. It's a sin to cover up those legs.' He grinned suddenly. 'Of course, I have to admit I miss the T-shirt, but I suppose I should try to keep my investors' minds on business some of the time.'

'I thought you were engaged to be married,' said Rachel.

'I *am* engaged to be married, but it hasn't affected my eyesight,' said Grant. 'It was an expression of purely aesthetic appreciation.' The blue eyes danced at Rachel's sceptical look. 'Which is more,' he added with a grimace, 'than I can express for this place. It's pretty chaotic, I'm afraid—one reason I'm so glad you can start today.

'There's a desk you can use somewhere under that pile of papers by the window, the phone's on the floor, there's a fax machine in the corner and a PC in a box in the next room—we'll be linked by network to the London office, obviously, but that's run into a couple of hitches, so you'll have to use it stand-alone for now. Sorry it's not already up and running, but I'll configure it for you as soon as you've got your desk sorted out so you can get down to work—'

'Oh, I'll take care of that,' said Rachel. 'And I'll see if I can't sort out the link with the network. Are you using a contractor? I can't imagine what the problem could be...'

'I know.' He shrugged. 'It's someone Olivia recommended, supposed to be as good as they come—I'll give you the details and you can see what you can get out of him.' He turned back to the table piled high with brochures. 'Oh, and I'll just give you the general picture about this place.'

He picked up a brochure and glowered at it.

'Basically, there are two stages to the project,' he told her. 'I've already got planning permission to use this place for conferences, so now we've just got to get it up and running—as soon as possible, obviously, so we can cover our costs and start turning a profit. The science park is a longer-term thing, because we've got to get clearance for something that's bound to have a much bigger impact, whether good or bad, on the area. The provisional deadline for getting the house ready is May, believe it or not, and if we could get some bookings for the summer so much the better.'

He slapped the brochure absent-mindedly against a thigh, and gave Rachel a rather rueful smile.

'The thing is, my main interest really is on the science-park side, specifically in getting a core of high-powered inventors who can bounce ideas off each other. I don't know much about conferences, to tell the truth; the centre was Olivia's idea. I think she's absolutely right in a lot of ways—good to give the place a high profile to attract the right people to the park, help with cash flow, and of course it will give us a fantastic base when we get married...'

Rachel felt her encouraging smile stiffen on her lips. 'Yes?' she said.

'But I don't have much of an idea what to aim at,' he confessed. 'I look through these things and it all seems so unnecessary. I mean, I once made a million dollars out of an idea I got from talking with a couple of people over a campfire, eating baked beans and drinking tea out of the tin the baked beans came in. Does anyone really need over-head projectors and felt display boards with Velcro attachments? But even I see that I can't offer people baked beans from the tin followed by bean-flavoured tea.'

He tossed a few catalogues to the ground and sat on the edge of the table, tossed a few more to the ground and gestured for Rachel to join him. 'I thought maybe we could put our heads together.'

Rachel stared at him.

'What is it?' He raised an eyebrow.

'You're not at all my idea of a self-made millionaire,' Rachel blurted out. It was odd the way she felt she could say anything to Grant. Somehow, she had to weigh every word when she talked to Driscoll, even if he was her fiancé.

'Really? Why? Is a profound respect for felt display boards with Velcro attachments supposed to come with the territory?'

Rachel shook her head. 'No, but—aren't you supposed to be steely-eyed and granite-jawed? Shouldn't you have a five-year plan? Shouldn't you be shouting at me for being five minutes late, or wearing too short a skirt—?'

'I won't hear a word against that skirt,' he interrupted.

'How could you just offer me a job on the spur of the moment? You should be grilling me on my qualifications— you didn't even ask me to take a typing test!' she said accusingly.

He considered a moment, absent-mindedly fanning the pages of the catalogue, then met her eyes with another of those quizzical smiles. Rachel didn't know how Olivia could be so impervious to them—Rachel could feel her own mouth smiling back, could even feel her pulse speeding up, and *she*, after all, was madly in love with Driscoll.

'Sorry, I suppose it must seem a bit haphazard.' The blue eyes were mildly amused. 'Well, it probably wouldn't hurt to get a few things straight.'

He drummed his fingers on the table-top. 'The thing is, the main thing you find out from any test is whether someone can pass the test. If you grill someone, you find out how they stand up to a grilling—but it's not much of a way to getting at what you really want to know, and you may have alienated a first-class worker before their first day on the job. In my experience what actually matters is how much somebody wants to do a job, and how good they are at getting what they want—of course skills matter, but they're secondary.'

He shrugged. 'Well, you were persistent, and prepared to go for the job under embarrassing circumstances, in the teeth of probable opposition from your fiancé—so the will was there. And you were apparently somebody who'd succeeded in getting an ordinary member of the public on first-name terms with a tarantula, so I reckoned you could find a way when you had the will. It was just a hunch, but my hunches usually work out pretty well—if you ask me, that's probably the thing self-made millionaires usually have in common.'

Rachel fought down an almost irresistible urge to ask if he'd had a hunch about Olivia. Or was she somebody else who'd wanted a job badly enough? Had Olivia convinced him she wanted the job of wife? But she'd seemed so perfunctory about everything but selecting the furniture! 'Well, I'll try to justify your faith in me,' she said primly instead.

He laughed. 'You already have. You look like a million dollars—definitely a credit to the firm. As for typing, I assume you wouldn't have wanted the job if you didn't have some knowledge of a keyboard. There won't be a huge amount to get through, so as long as the finished product looks all right I don't care whether you type a hundred words a minute or use the fast three-finger method.'

'And what if I don't work out?' Rachel persisted, oddly curious.

'Oh, I'll just have to practise looking steely-eyed when I shave. Seriously, though—if you're not up to the job I'll have to get someone else in; it's as simple as that—and I can certainly show someone the door if I have to. But even then I'd still think I could've made a more expensive mistake using some big recruitment agency that gave spelling tests and typing tests and couldn't see the potential in a girl with a way with spiders.'

He opened the catalogue again and gestured beside him. 'So there you have it,' he said, with another of those knee-weakening grins. 'The secret of my success. But my Achilles' heel is a complete lack of sympathy for office or any other furniture—so any advice you can give will be more than welcome.'

Rachel hesitated, then hopped up to sit beside him on the table and look down at the furniture portrayed in the glossy pages. Suddenly her skirt seemed a lot shorter, she realised; an endless expanse of gleaming, Lycra-clad leg seemed to swing over the edge of the table. And Grant, suddenly, seemed not just close but disturbingly close. Their knees were almost touching; he'd put the catalogue on her lap now, and leant over her shoulder to inspect it. She could see the smooth, clean line of his jaw, the ash-dark hair cut close to the skull around his ear, shading the bright gleam of hair that had been burnished by the sun.

'Is something the matter?' he asked, the brilliant blue eyes meeting hers. 'I'm really not a hard taskmaster, you know.'

Rachel shook her head.

His eyes dropped to the page again. 'I don't know,' he said gloomily. 'This all seems so unnecessary. Do you know anything about conferences?'

He stretched out a hand to turn a page, accidentally brushing Rachel's arm. She felt as if an electric shock had suddenly run up her arm; in her confusion she forgot that too much knowledge was a dangerous thing.

'Oh, yes,' she said, 'I know all about conferences. You really don't need to worry about all this paraphernalia—I mean, you need enough to look respectable, but it's not the main thing.' She was speaking rapidly to distract herself from his closeness now—saying the first thing that came into her head.

'The thing you've got to remember is that the papers aren't really the point—they're an excuse. The overhead projectors are just to make it look like a good excuse. The big names will come and give papers they've put together in three days—they won't waste time doing something big for a mere conference—and shoals of minor people will give things they've cobbled together to get a publication record.'

'You're very cynical, Spidergirl,' he told her. 'If you're right, it's hardly worth doing at all, is it? I might as well turn the place into an adventure park.'

Rachel shook her head. 'Not necessarily,' she assured him. 'The point of it all is—it's sort of like giving people a chance to have those conversations you had over a campfire drinking tea from a tin. Nobody's going to pay an airfare to let someone sit by a campfire and eat baked beans, whereas people can get funding to go to a conference, especially if they're giving a paper. And once they're there—with a bit of luck—some sparks might fly.'

She flicked the catalogue dismissively. 'Of course a lot of it's just people promoting their careers, but a few ideas can come out of it. So the crucial thing is to make it easy for people to socialise outside the papers. Keep the bar or, better, bars open as long as you can. Have lots of little nooks where a few people can sit over coffee. Make it easy to get refreshments in an informal way any time of the day or night. Get that right and, frankly, no one will care whether you've got Velcro or Sellotape on your felt-backed boards.'

It was only when she reached the end of this little speech that she realised that Grant was looking at her oddly.

'You seem to know a lot about it,' he remarked. 'I thought there was more to you than meets the eye.'

'Oh...' said Rachel. 'I lived in a university town for

several years,' she explained, perfectly truthfully. 'I helped out at a lot of conferences.' Mainly by giving papers, but never mind that.

'I see,' said Grant. He smiled. 'I tried to go to a conference once. R. K. V. Hawkins was giving a paper on insect populations in the pampas. Then a crisis blew up at work and I missed him. But I refuse to believe it was just something R. K. V. threw together for the airfare.'

Before Rachel could think of a suitable reply to this the telephone rang. She looked wildly around; the sound seemed to be coming from a mound of papers in the corner.

'I'll get it!' they both exclaimed, leaping from the table. This was a mistake.

The smooth soles of Rachel's brand new shoes skidded on one of the brochures which had been tossed to the floor; Grant's beautifully polished black loafers slipped on another. They toppled headlong to the ground.

Grant reached out a long arm and extracted the telephone from beneath the pile of papers. 'Arrowmead Conference Centre,' he said, as imperturbably as if he'd been sitting behind a twelve by ten black marble desk instead of entangled on the floor with a breathless secretary. 'Oh—yes, she's right here.'

'It's for you,' he said to Rachel, handing over the receiver.

Rachel held it to her ear.

'Hello?' she said. 'Oh, hello, Driscoll.'

Grant had been on the point of sitting up, but he now simply propped himself on one elbow and gave her a lazy grin. 'Tell him he's a lucky man,' he said. 'Tell him if he tries to interfere with your career he'll have me to reckon with.'

Rachel frowned. 'No, it's nothing, Driscoll—no, I—yes, I thought I'd give it a try—yes, I realise it's a departure, but I—I really don't think this is the time to discuss this.'

Driscoll ignored her. 'Look, Rache, something big has

come up. You got a letter from Bell Conglomerates—they want you to do an environmental impact study for them—plenty of scope for both of us.'

'You opened it?' said Rachel.

'Of course I opened it. It could have been important. It *is* important. There's not a moment to lose.'

'But I'm not interested,' protested Rachel.

Driscoll argued vehemently. At last, he said reluctantly, 'Well, if you don't want it, maybe I'll apply on my own. Tell you what, why don't we both go to London in person? Then you can put in a good word for me—you know, say you're definitely not interested and that I'm the next best thing.'

Rachel hesitated. Driscoll had never been much of a one for fieldwork. Would he be able to do an independent survey if it turned out one was needed? But there was Grant's philosophy, she reminded herself—and Driscoll certainly wanted the job badly.

'Well, all right,' she said at last. 'When do you want to go?'

'They've given you an appointment for Wednesday next week.'

'I'll see if I can make it,' Rachel said reluctantly.

Grant was still looking at her, the brilliant blue eyes watchful. 'Now, don't tell me he's talked you into quitting on your first day on the job,' he said.

Rachel shook her head. 'I'm afraid you won't like it, though,' she said hesitantly. 'I've got to go up to London on Wednesday next week.'

Grant shrugged. 'As a matter of fact, so have I. I'll give you a lift, shall I? That way I can make sure you come back.'

CHAPTER FOUR

In the week before her appointment Rachel brought order to the chaotic office. She managed, through sheer obstinate perseverance, to get through on the phone to the firm handling the network, and got the computers connected to the London headquarters. She set up a filing system. She made a number of recommendations about requirements for the conference centre. She also spent a surprising amount of time talking with her eccentric, easygoing employer about things that seemed to have nothing to do with business.

Though Grant had abandoned an orthodox scientific career, he still had an active, wide-ranging interest in an extraordinary variety of scientific subjects. The reception area was soon piled high with periodicals he pretended to think visitors might like to consult. He seemed to be unable to visit a bookshop without bringing away five or six things that 'looked interesting'; this was his explanation, at any rate, for the large number of books that soon cluttered his office. He encouraged Rachel to borrow anything she liked; then he argued with her about it.

This was not, of course, for the most part in office hours. Olivia had gone back to London, since the upstairs was still uninhabitable. That didn't stop Grant from camping out there—it just meant he had his evenings free. Just as Rachel was getting ready to leave for the day, he'd come in and ask a casual question about something she'd been reading. The next thing she knew three or four hours would have gone by.

One night he might bundle her into the Jaguar and take her off to a three-star country restaurant. On another he'd remember he had a couple of tins of baked beans and a carton of eggs upstairs. Either way, Rachel realised she hadn't had such a good time in years. Grant had a knack for spotting what was original and interesting in new work; it was wonderful talking with him! In fact, she sometimes thought guiltily, she couldn't remember the last time she'd talked about new developments in any field with Driscoll. Driscoll talked about the jobs that were going, and who was likely to get them. Well, of course you had to be practical, but it was wonderfully refreshing to talk to someone who was just interested in the subject.

If she was honest, Rachel had to admit that there was more to it than the thrill of discussing the latest developments in DNA research. She'd never spent so much time in the company of such a spectacular physical specimen, and there was no point in pretending she didn't enjoy it. A fact was a fact, and as a scientist Rachel had a great respect for facts.

There was also no point in pretending she didn't enjoy going into the office and getting a daily expression of aesthetic appreciation from said spectacular physical specimen. It was just a joke, of course, but it cheered her up anyway. The mosquitoes had never had much time for aesthetics: they'd just gone for blood.

Since he was engaged, and she was engaged, it was a lucky thing that there was no danger of her falling in love with Grant. He didn't always talk about science. Sometimes he talked instead about hair-raising escapes he'd had.

Rachel didn't know whether Olivia knew what she was getting into; maybe she didn't believe she would ever personally be in danger. Rachel knew better. She might get short of breath sometimes at a certain look in those blazing blue eyes, she might sometimes feel her pulse quicken when he stood close to her—it didn't matter. All it took was one blood-chilling reminiscence to expose these for the trifling physical phenomena they were. This man was trouble. Rachel did not like trouble. Therefore, this man was emphatically not her type.

Still, even if she didn't want to marry him, she couldn't imagine a more delightful, stimulating employer. This was the job for her. By the end of the week she was even more reluctant to accept the environmental assessment assignment.

The Tuesday night before the fateful interview was another three-star restaurant night. Grant came into the front office at five-thirty, finger in the middle of a book on alternative medicine, paced up and down for two or three hours talking heatedly about various questions it raised, and suddenly remembered he was starving. Rachel had told her aunt days before that she couldn't count on being home in time for dinner; she was now able to rush down to the Jaguar with Grant without even an apologetic phone call.

Half an hour of expert driving through the country lanes brought them to one of the most famous restaurants in the county. Another fifteen minutes and they were devouring an appetiser of roasted vegetables while they argued about genetic engineering. Rachel had been thinking all day about the interview, and then trying not to think about it. Now, as she gazed across the candlelit table at Grant's blazing eyes and infectious smile, she decided for the fifteenth time that day not to think about the interview but just to enjoy herself while she could. And just as she'd reached this sensible decision she looked across the room, and saw Olivia at a table with a group of stylishly dressed older people.

Grant's eyes followed hers. Rachel wondered for a moment whether he would mind being found having dinner tête-à-tête with another woman, but Grant seemed to have other things on his mind.

'Oh, no,' he groaned. 'Did you see what I just saw?'

'Olivia?' hazarded Rachel.

'My fiancée, yes,' he agreed. 'And, more to the point, my fiancée in the bosom of her family, and, as if that weren't bad enough, in the company of her family's friends. Well, we can't pretend we haven't seen them—we might as well get this over with. Come on.'

He stood up and escorted Rachel to the other table, where he performed introductions with an unusually subdued manner. 'You remember Rachel,' he told Olivia.

Olivia's eyes widened. It was clear that she hadn't recognised the scruffy spider-catcher in the dark-haired, beautifully groomed girl with Grant.

'Of course,' she said smoothly. 'And you remember Rupert, of course.'

'Of course,' Grant said. He glowered at the distinguished, silver-haired man to Olivia's right. 'Rachel, I'd like you to meet Rupert Matheson, managing director of Glomac. Rupert—my secretary, Rachel.'

Matheson extended a beautifully manicured hand and shook Rachel's. 'Delighted,' he murmured. 'You'll join us for a drink, of course.' He pulled over a chair for Rachel before Grant could demur; Grant drew up a chair for himself and sat down with evident reluctance.

Matheson seemed somewhat amused by Grant's ill-concealed distaste. 'How are you getting on with raising funds for the science park?' he asked.

'Well enough,' Grant said curtly.

'It's not easy sometimes for a small operation like yours,' Matheson commented. Rachel stared at him in astonishment, then remembered that Glomac was one of the largest pharmaceuticals companies in the world.

'I don't see any problem,' said Grant. 'Of course it's early days. The environmental impact assessment should be pretty straightforward, but obviously we've got to deal with a few formalities before we really get going.'

'Quite, quite,' agreed the older man. 'Well, you've got a marvellous location. We may be interested ourselves.'

Grant merely raised an eyebrow.

'And if the investors don't come as fast as you'd hoped...' Matheson paused and took a sip of his drink '...you might reconsider leasing the rights we spoke of. You know Glomac can develop the product on a much bigger scale; it would be worth our while to make it well worth your while.'

Grant drained his glass and set it down. 'Thanks, but I don't think so,' he said. 'I'm afraid we'll have to leave you; our dinner has come.'

He stood up and stalked back to the other table, Rachel trailing behind him in perplexity.

'A bigger scale,' Grant said tightly. 'Couldn't they just. My God, he makes me sick.' His face was black.

'What was he talking about?' Rachel asked.

'I helped an Amazonian tribe to get some land rights a few years back. Now I've got an agreement with them to research and develop use of some of the native plants as medicines—there's one that looks like it might be the next wonder drug.' He gave her a grim smile. 'Well, naturally Glomac would love to get its hands on it. More specifically, Matheson would love to be able to chalk up a spectacular money-spinner to himself—the company's been stagnating since he took charge.'

'And you don't trust him?'

Grant shrugged. 'He can't afford to deal fairly with the tribe. To make the kind of money he wants, he'd have to get them off the land. They've had enough contact with civilisation so that they don't have the kind of cash-independent existence they once had; Glomac would refuse to pay them a decent price for the product until they were desperate, then offer them an attractive deal to sell the land outright. I'm not saying Matheson would admit in so many words that it was acceptable for the tribe to end up in the slums of Recife, provided Glomac made enough money out of it, but he'd look the other way while it happened.'

He glanced contemptuously across the room. 'It's not easy for Olivia,' he added. 'He's a friend of her father, so she can't really cut the acquaintance.'

'I see,' said Rachel noncommittally. She took a sip of wine. It didn't seem to her that Olivia's friendliness to the man had been forced, but this was hardly something she could say to Grant.

The sparkle and spontaneity of their conversation seemed to have been quenched by the short visit to the other table. They ate quickly, not saying much; neither felt like lingering over dessert or coffee, and they left by mutual consent after another twenty minutes.

Rachel got into the car the next morning in a gloomy mood. Even Grant's enthusiastic reunion with the pink suit failed to raise her spirits. If *only* Bell Conglomerates would listen to reason and take Driscoll instead. But would they?

The drive to London passed largely in silence. Grant seemed preoccupied by the encounter of the previous evening; Rachel was full of foreboding at the prospect of her interview. The more she thought about it, the less she thought Bell Conglomerates was going to take a substitute on her say-so. If she wasn't careful, they'd suck her back into fieldwork before she could bat an eye—they'd sponsored her graduate work, after all, and might try to make her feel she owed them one.

That was problem number one. The second problem was her hair, or lack thereof. She still hadn't broken the news to Driscoll—what if the shock put him off his stride? What if it lowered her credibility as a reference with Bell Conglomerates?

Well, she could do nothing about problem number one, but she could spare Driscoll's sensibilities. She asked Grant to drop her off in Oxford Street, bought a shoulder-length black wig in Selfridges, and had plenty of time to arrange this artfully on her head before setting off to meet Driscoll.

It wasn't exactly her usual style, but Driscoll wasn't exactly the noticing type.

They met in the lobby of Bell. Driscoll didn't notice the wig. He did notice, and disapproved of, the pink suit, which he thought had too short a skirt. He explained that he'd confirmed the appointment in her name with the head of the company.

They went to the top floor, and were shown to a reception area outside the director's office. Driscoll stood, hands clasped behind his back, looking out of the window; Rachel sat leafing through an old copy of *Nature*. Footsteps came bounding down the corridor.

'Hawkins!' exclaimed a familiar voice. 'This is a real pleasure—I can't tell you how glad I am to meet you at last. Terrific that you'll be working for us. Won't you come into my office?'

Under Rachel's bemused stare, none other than Grant Mallett advanced on Driscoll and shook him heartily by the hand. A handshake was insufficiently cordial to express the intensity of his delight; he slapped him even more heartily on the back, then steered him through the door of the office. The door closed behind them.

Rachel expected them to bounce out again immediately, but the door remained shut for some time. Presently it opened again. Driscoll's face was flushed; Grant's, she was surprised to see, was uncharacteristically grim.

'I'm afraid that's not the way I do business,' he said. 'But, in any case, I particularly want Hawkins for this job, and as it was one of the conditions of the Bell grant that the recipient be prepared to do something of the kind there's really nothing to be discussed. If you've brought Dr Hawkins with you I'll have a word now—' He broke off, and looked blankly about the reception area, then at Rachel, then around the room again, as if a stray zoologist might be hiding under a sofa, and then back, again, at Rachel.

'Rachel?' he said. He gave her a rather preoccupied

smile. 'I'd know that suit anywhere, but why, in God's name, the wig?' Before she could answer, he did a sudden double take, and looked again at Driscoll. 'Oh, my God,' he said. 'You don't mean...?'

'Yes,' Rachel said resignedly.

'Your fiancé,' said Grant. 'Driscoll. I should have known there couldn't be two. I'm sorry not to have better news for you both,' he said, with painstaking politeness, 'but I've someone else in mind for the job. Any idea where Hawkins might have gone?' He flicked a glance at Driscoll. 'I'd like to get this sorted out today.'

Driscoll stared at him. 'I've already explained,' he said rather sulkily, 'that Rachel is not interested in the work. If you don't believe me, ask her.'

There was a short silence. Grant looked at Driscoll. 'Rachel?' he said.

'She would rather not take on any more fieldwork,' said Driscoll. 'I understand she's working as your secretary down in the country; I think it's a waste, but it's what she prefers, and I can't see why you won't accept her recommendation for someone to take her place.'

Grant looked at Rachel. 'Dr Hawkins?' he said. 'Dr R. K. V. Hawkins?'

Rachel sighed.

'Let's go into my office,' Grant said grittily. 'We have a few things to discuss.'

He stalked into the office, holding the door for Rachel, then slammed it behind them.

'How could you?' he growled.

'How could I what?' said Rachel, trying not to think of Driscoll stranded in Reception. Something told her that Driscoll would not appreciate this chance to catch up on missed issues of *Nature* and *National Geographic*.

'I don't know where to begin,' said Grant, pacing up and down and glaring at her. 'Wear that wig? Take the damned thing off, will you? Entertain for even two minutes the thought of marrying that unconscionable prat? Throw away a brilliant scientific career to advise me on how many bars to have, and whether to have a vending machine for biscuits? *Pretend*,' he roared, 'that you'd never heard of R. K. V. Hawkins?'

'If you weren't so sexist you wouldn't have assumed it was a man,' Rachel retorted. 'And then you'd have made the connection yourself.'

'What connection?' snapped Grant. 'Your uncle's last name is Bright. It didn't occur to me—'

'That my aunt might be my mother's sister,' Rachel completed helpfully.

'You're right,' said Grant. 'In fact, you're right about everything. I *should* grill prospective secretaries. Then I could squeeze out of them closely guarded secrets, like their last names. Next time some scientific genius comes along professing a little knowledge of scientific terminology I won't waste money on a clothes allowance. You must have laughed your head off.'

'Of course I didn't,' Rachel protested, suppressing a smile. 'Well, only a little,' she admitted. 'But I was so tired of fieldwork. I wanted to work in an artificially controlled environment. I thought if I told you who I was you'd make me stand in some wretched swamp,' she concluded bitterly.

Grant thrust his hands in his pockets. He smiled reluctantly. 'I'm afraid I've got to go,' he said. 'Sorry, R. K. V., but you're definitely the man for the job.'

'You told me never to wear jeans again,' said Rachel.

'You'll have to waste some of your assets whatever you do—and no sacrifice is too great in the cause of science.'

Rachel sighed. She leant gloomily against the side of his desk, this time an immense block of glass and black marble which was about what you'd expect of a millionaire and company director. Gloomily she crossed her ankles and stared down at the long, Lycra-clad legs so soon to be encased in muddy jeans and wellington boots.

'You still haven't taken off your wig,' said Grant. He came to her side and plucked it off unceremoniously. 'I can't believe you wanted to cover this up,' he told her. 'Was that for Driscoll's benefit? It's lovely. I can never see it without wanting to touch it.'

He ran a finger through the short sooty hair. Rachel shivered.

'And you haven't told me how you came to be engaged to that nincompoop,' said Grant.

'He is *not*,' said Rachel. 'He's everything you want me to be—methodical, painstaking...'

'He's a plodder,' Grant said ruthlessly. 'Coasting along behind a sprinter. He sounded bad enough, but now that I've seen him it's out of the question. You can't marry him.'

'Why not?' Rachel said furiously.

'Because,' said Grant, 'he doesn't kiss you like this.'

CHAPTER FIVE

RAIN poured from a leaden sky, lashing the lake, whipping through the reedbeds like bullets and cascading down the willow trees which lined the shore. Her rubber-booted legs thigh-high in the water, Rachel stared morosely under the brim of a yellow sou'wester at the various areas she had marked for observation.

It had been two months since her interview in Grant's office. She'd tried to throw herself with grim determination into the environmental impact study; not for the first time, she was unable to concentrate, unable to think of anything but that shocking kiss.

That was the maddening thing. It had been just a kiss, after all. What was a kiss? Nothing. A casual physical contact, soon over, soon forgotten. Or it *should* have been. That was why she hadn't tried to get away—it had seemed to be making too much of a trifle.

At least, that was what she'd told herself at the time, though now she was beginning to wonder. She didn't know who she was angrier with, herself or Grant. No, she did know, she decided, her blue eyes smouldering as she remembered some of the things Grant had said. He was absolutely insufferable! Worst of all, and most unfairly, he had also made her—well, not exactly angry, but annoyed with Driscoll.

Rachel scowled at the rainswept lake. The problem was that Grant was right. Driscoll had all kinds of sterling qualities that Grant did not, though just at the moment she was

having trouble remembering them, but a kiss from Driscoll
was not an event. It was something you might do if you'd
nothing better to do—and Driscoll usually thought she did
have something better to do, like writing up research; it
was something to get out of the way before going on to do
something more interesting; it was completely unmemora-
ble. In fact, she couldn't remember the last time Driscoll
had kissed her. Whereas even two months later she could
remember every single sizzling second… Rachel closed her
eyes. She could almost feel it even now…

He gripped her arms at the shoulders, not gently, holding
her pinned against the desk, and for a split second he stood
looking down into her face. She could have ducked, or
twisted away, but instead she stared, mesmerised, into those
brilliant blue eyes, their colour as deep and clear as a Greek
sea—something so spectacular you thought it had to have
been touched up in the travel posters until you saw the real
thing—and somehow the sheer intensity of his gaze seemed
to deepen the impossible colour even further.

She thought she might have been able to push aside the
steely-eyed magnate of her imagination, but his was a kind
of power against which she seemed to have no defence.
The thick black lashes fringing his eyes, the black hooks
of his eyebrows were now implacably level across his forehead; the lock of burnished hair which had fallen forward
into his face… Seen so close, the sheer masculine beauty
had a potency which was intoxicating. And in that split
second she realised something she'd tried to ignore ever
since she'd seen him in the antique shop, ever since she'd
seen his face bent to Olivia's—that she'd wondered what
it would be like to be kissed by someone of such overwhelming physical magnetism.

And then his mouth was on hers.

She didn't know what she'd expected—maybe the ruthless kiss of a granite-jawed tycoon, the kind of kiss that

would make you want to land a punch on the granite jaw as soon as it was over. It wasn't like that at all. It was much, much worse. Or better.

The touch of his lips seemed to scorch hers, as if just that simple contact was a match that sent flame licking along the edge of a sheet of paper. His mouth was insistent, demanding—but it was the startling, unbearable sweetness of that first contact which forced her mouth open, as if, having so much—so little—she had to have more. She opened her mouth hungrily, and her knees weakened— she'd never realised a man could *taste* so good. In fact he tasted the way he looked—*unbelievably* good. Driscoll's kisses were wet, but she couldn't remember their tasting of anything—it was as if she'd been eating wet cardboard all her life.

She shouldn't be thinking about that. She shouldn't think about Driscoll when Grant was kissing her. In fact she couldn't really think of anything at all except, in a little corner of her mind, that Grant had obviously spent a lot of time improving on his natural advantages. Whatever you might think of his morals—and she'd have a lot to say about them at some stage—his technique was out of this world. His tongue was exploring her mouth, at first tracing, with a delicacy that made her shudder involuntarily, the line of her own tongue—then playing with it, tantalising her— then plunging deep within.

He wasn't holding her, at this stage, with even one hand. Then he raised one hand to cradle her head, the fingers grazing the short silky hair with a touch so light that it was barely perceptible, yet so sensuous that it made her scalp prickle with sudden awareness. His other hand cupped her jaw, the strong thumb lightly stroking the delicate skin. And still his mouth was on hers, demanding, giving…and instead of taking advantage of this opening to punch him, or stamp on his feet, or kick his shins, if only out of common loyalty to Driscoll, she realised that she had always wanted to touch that gleaming hair; she raised one hand to his head and buried her fingers in it.

It was thick, and soft, like the fur of some beautiful animal. She stroked it, and he drew in his breath sharply. She realised that she had always wanted to run a hand along the smooth skin of his jaw, and suddenly nothing was simpler than to raise her other hand to his face. He leant into her hand for a moment, as if in spontaneous delight at her touch; somehow his evident pleasure in the taste of her mouth, in the touch of her hand made her own pleasure even more acute—as if she was learning from him how much pleasure it was possible to take.

And it was at this moment that Rachel made a discovery: she shouldn't have let Grant kiss her when she was engaged to Driscoll, she should have fought him off, but, since she had and she hadn't, the only thing she wanted was for it to go on as long as possible. There were lots of things in life more important than sex, and she and Driscoll had all of them in common. No responsible adult would sacrifice all those things just because she couldn't expect kisses like strong, straight liquor. And since she was never going to kiss anyone like this again she might as well make the most of it.

Leaving one hand buried in his hair, the better to force his head back down if he should for some reason try to raise it, Rachel put her other arm around his waist, holding him close to her. She had just an instant to appreciate the hard muscle under her hand, so different from the layer of flab on the average academic; then his arms were around her, gripping her tightly. For one white-hot moment they seemed to devour each other—and then he dropped his arms and shook himself loose.

Rachel stared up at him. He was breathing hard, and staring at her with an odd expression. She was in no condition to analyse it but it did not seem much like the look of someone about to say, Told you so. If anything, he looked appalled. Strange, when he'd certainly enjoyed it every bit as much as she had—but then she wasn't really in a condition to think very clearly; she was, she knew, staring up at him with naked longing.

His eyes were as blue as sapphires; his mouth was still moist. Involuntarily she ran her tongue over her lips. He seemed to move involuntarily towards her, then catch himself. His mouth tightened.

'You're so—beautiful,' said Rachel, staring at him.

'I think that's my line,' said Grant. He thrust his hands in his pockets as if they might start something if he didn't put them out of the way. 'Anyway,' he said, 'you see what I mean. You can't marry him.'

Rachel sighed, and drifted slowly back down to earth. 'Of course I can,' she said firmly. 'There's more to life than sex, Grant. There are more important things, like intellectual compatibility, and shared interests, and—and mutual respect.'

'*What?*'

'A good marriage needs a solid foundation, which is exactly what I have in my relationship with Driscoll. You have to be adult about these things, Grant; you can't expect life to be ideal; you have to be prepared to compromise. You can't just throw away the things that really matter, just because someone happens to be physically attractive—'

'I don't believe I'm hearing this,' said Grant. He ran his hands exasperatedly back through his hair, completing the general chaos begun there by Rachel. 'Of course intellectual compatibility matters. I'm not saying you should marry someone without it. But if that's *all* you've got, why get married? Why not just collaborate on a paper, or swap offprints? What does it take to make you see that?'

'It would take a lot more than one little kiss,' she snapped.

'*Really?*' He raised a sardonic eyebrow. 'Is that a proposition? How far do you want to go?'

'Of all the arrogant, self-satisfied, sex-obsessed idiots,' said Rachel, 'you take the cake. I suppose you think I should go to bed with you just for the sake of comparison.'

'Not at all. You've never slept with him, so you'd have nothing to compare with.'

Rachel gritted her teeth. 'What makes you say that?'

'It's obvious. You couldn't even think of marrying him if you had. In fact I'm beginning to think you can't have slept with anyone.'

Rachel could feel blood rushing to her cheeks. 'I have so,' she said furiously. His sceptical look infuriated her even more; it might not actually be true, but he could at least have the decency to take her word for it. 'I've had *lots* of lovers,' she added extravagantly.

'Intellectually compatible incompetents to a man, by the looks of it,' he said drily. 'No, don't.' He cut off before she could manufacture marvels of prowess for these figments of the imagination. He spread his hands wide in a sudden gesture of appeal. 'Look, I've said—done—this all wrong. You don't have to prove anything to me. All I'm saying is that you seem to be deliberately turning your back on one of the most wonderful things in the world, and all out of some bone-headed idea of maturity.'

He looked at her steadily. 'I thought you were pretty spectacular even when I thought you were just an over-qualified secretary with a sideline in tarantula-taming. Now it turns out you've a brilliant mind as well. You could have any man you want. I can't stand the thought of someone so beautiful and alive burying it all because she doesn't know what she's missing. I didn't mean to be arrogant; I just thought I could show you—I thought I had shown you—a side of yourself that you seemed to be ignoring. I'm sorry it's made you so angry; I just wanted to spare you a lifetime of frustration.'

Rachel had no time to digest the fact that Grant Mallett, of all people, thought she could have any man she wanted;

she was too furious. 'Are you sure you weren't reminding
yourself of a side of yourself you'd been overlooking?' she
asked acidly. 'Maybe *you're* the one who's frustrated. Your
fiancée doesn't seem exactly responsive.'

'We'll leave Olivia out of this.'

'So you haven't made any compromises. You're madly
in love and blissfully happy and you just go around kissing
other women out of pure altruism,' Rachel said sarcastically.

'I wouldn't say "pure" exactly,' he said with a reluctant
smile. There was a glimmer of amusement in the brilliant
blue eyes, though his expression was still sombre. 'Why do
I feel as if I were some insect population under analysis?
Let's just forget about it, R. K. V. There's got to be some
cliché to cover the situation. You were breathtakingly beautiful, I had an irresistible urge and lost my head, you're too
sensible to organise your life around irresistible urges—
over to you, Dr Hawkins.'

Rachel glared at him; how dared he call an end to the
fight just when she was beginning to land a few punches?

'I've got your new contract and details of the parts of
the environmental impact assessment that will be your responsibility. I think the only thing we need to worry about
is the southwest corner—there are some pretty extensive
reedbeds which might need to be handled with care—but
obviously you'll need to make up your own mind.'

He reached over to the desk, picked up a large brown
envelope and placed it in her hands. 'I've put Steve Phillips
in charge of the non-ecological side: he's had a lot of experience with social impact assessments, which was what
was mainly at issue when we got planning permission for
the conference centre. You should talk to him in the next
week or so. Other than that, you've got a free hand in
putting together your own team.'

He raised an eyebrow. 'I realise you can't be expected
to be an expert in every relevant aspect of the ecology, so

you'll probably need support from specialists outside your own field. Since your friend's work overlaps so closely with yours, though, I'd be surprised if the project required his professional services.'

Rachel was so demoralised that even the word 'reedbed' didn't make her flinch.

A crack of lightning split the sky. The rain began to come down with less violence, but in a steady downpour which could obviously go on for hours. The wind howled. It was not going to be possible to carry out her weekly observation of the sector when she couldn't see anything more than three inches from her nose.

Rachel sighed. The Department of the Environment guidelines said optimistically that most environmental assessments should require no new scientific research. Rachel herself had never worked on a project where everyone hadn't started out assuming that no new research would need to be done. After all, a wealth of information was available from organisations ranging from the water authorities to the Royal Society for the Protection of Birds.

It was only after you'd spent a few months going through all that information that you realised that some of it was out of date, or that the observers had used such different survey methods that the data couldn't be correlated and that you would need to carry out further research.

She had gone through the same routine this time. To do Grant justice, she hadn't spent the whole of the last two months in an aquatic environment. Apart from a few meetings with Grant and her new colleague, Phillips, Rachel had spent most of the time working sixteen-hour days seven days a week, going through sheafs and sheafs of reports and statistics on the ecology of the area.

The problem was that if new research had to be done, the period between May and September was crucial for making observations. At the end of the day, of course, she'd discovered that the reedbeds had grown up in the last ten or fifteen or twenty years—it wasn't always easy to tell from the reports, which focused on different things—that they had never been systematically studied, and that she was going to have to spend a significant amount of time more or less submerged.

By working at breakneck speed Rachel had managed to determine the need for further research by the third week in April—just in time to set herself up for a whole summer's worth of fieldwork. After just a week in the field she'd made an important discovery. She should, she realised now, have taken longer coffee-breaks.

Rachel sloshed back to shore. The reedbeds weren't the only thing that needed further research, but she wouldn't be able to see anything else any better in this rain. If she couldn't carry out any more observations today, she reasoned, she might as well go by the house and bring her paperwork up to date. No need to see Grant, who probably wasn't there anyway—and even if he was she didn't see why *she* should have to avoid *him*.

She got on her bicycle and began weaving her way unsteadily along the softened dirt of the access road.

The fact was, she thought, brooding darkly, that she probably would have forgotten the kiss—well, at least put it behind her—well, anyway, only thought about it a couple of times a week—if Driscoll had behaved differently. He'd sulked all the way through dinner that night, complaining over and over again about the humiliation of his interview with Grant. Mallett had said this, and Driscoll should have said that, and Mallet had said this, and all Driscoll could think of to say had been that.

It had occurred to Rachel, uncomfortably, that she'd spent an awful lot of the last six years listening to post-mortems of unfair exams and bad interviews, soothing Driscoll's ego and assuring him that he was brilliant and sure to get something soon and that it probably hadn't been as bad as he'd thought.

Then she'd thought she was being unfair. The ivory tower was a figment of the imagination of people who had nothing to do with the academic world. Academia was as much a rat race as anywhere else, and good people often didn't do well. She was probably feeling unsympathetic for completely different reasons.

What with her travel for fieldwork, and the frenzy of writing up her own research and helping Driscoll to write up his, they'd never really had the chance to become physically close. That was probably why she'd felt so remote watching Driscoll stuff chips into his mouth while he complained about Mallett. The feeling of remoteness had infuriated her; she'd felt as if Grant was looking over her shoulder murmuring, Told you so. Well, she'd show him, she'd thought. At the first break in Driscoll's monologue she'd suggested they spend the night together in a London hotel.

Now, Driscoll had always been preoccupied with work. He'd never seemed to feel he could spare much time for anything else, and he'd never shown much interest in even the mild lovemaking they'd engaged in up till then. It hadn't been fair to expect him to reverse the habits of a lifetime and show the kind of enthusiasm Grant would probably have shown at such a suggestion. Rachel had had to admit, though, that she'd expected something better than what she'd got: Driscoll had just looked irritated at the interruption, then continued where he'd left off.

'Maybe it would help to take your mind off this,' said Rachel, feeling less and less enthusiastic. Still, at least *she* was *trying*.

'Don't be ridiculous,' Driscoll said impatiently. 'Anyway, what would we do about contraception?'

'Isn't there a late-night chemist at Marble Arch? You could get something there…'

'*What?*' Driscoll turned bright red. 'Go into a *chemist*? There might be a girl at the till.'

It seemed to Rachel that this coyness was rather out of place in a zoologist, but she said impatiently, 'All right, I'll go in.'

Driscoll sighed—a long, deep, put-upon sigh. 'I'm really not in the mood, Rachel,' he said. 'I'd have thought you could see that. And anyway, I've got another interview tomorrow. I'm going to need my sleep. I don't know what's got into you, Rachel; we've already discussed this on numerous occasions. Neither of us needs our intellectual productivity disrupted. It's preposterous to jeopardise our careers with the kind of turmoil sexual activity could bring.'

Well, maybe he had a point, Rachel thought grimly now, cycling through the rain. Considering the turmoil she'd been in for the past two months just because of one stupid kiss, maybe he was right. But Grant's words had come, unnervingly pat, into her mind. 'Why get married? Why not just swap offprints?' For one unthinkable moment she'd even thought of saying it—of saying it, what was more, to a man who'd just had the worst interview of his life.

She'd been so horrified by this evidence of her nasty, selfish nature that she'd been unusually sympathetic for the rest of the evening. She hadn't been able to help being aware of the strain this had put her under, probably because of her nasty, selfish nature. That, unfortunately, had made her even angrier with Grant, whom she could imagine saying, Told you so. And the fact that Driscoll had remained sublimely unaware of the effort she was making had made her even more annoyed with Driscoll.

It had been almost a relief to get back to the country, go through the paperwork and find she'd have to get her teeth into a solid stint of fieldwork.

Almost. Rachel toiled up the rutted access road, which was now cutting its way up a slope. Rain sprayed her face and dripped down her chin. She reached the top of the hill

and wobbled down the other side, and for a moment was
torn by envy of the lucky girl who was ensconced, at this
very moment, in the dry, carpeted office which was to have
been Rachel's domain.

In the moment of envy her attention left the road, to be
brought back, abruptly, by the roar of a four-wheel-drive
vehicle flying down the hill towards her. The access road
was too narrow for two, too wet and muddy for sudden
stops, and in the pouring rain—especially as it hadn't occurred to her to put her lights on—the bicycle was probably
invisible.

The access road was lined by thick bushes here. The first
break was close to the bottom of the slope. Gritting her
teeth, Rachel pedalled furiously, bucketing down the ruts
of the road. She reached the bottom just ahead of the vehicle.

There was no time for thought. With a wrench of the
handles, Rachel shot off the side of the road and into a
convenient, rainwater-filled ditch.

CHAPTER SIX

'RACHEL? Rachel! Are you all right?'

Rachel would have known that voice anywhere. In fact, she decided, staggering to her feet in four feet of dirty water and dragging her bicycle up from the depths, she should have known who the driver was even without the voice.

'Rachel?' said Grant. To give him his due, he'd actually got out of the car. He was standing at the side of the road, about six feet above her head. 'Do you need help getting back up?'

'Just a minute,' said Rachel. Her interest had been caught by a clump of yellow iris a few feet away.

With a mighty shove, she heaved the bicycle out of the water and left it on its side above the waterline. Dirty water was pouring *out* of the sleeves and neck of her yellow plastic mac; well, she couldn't get any wetter than she already was. Rachel struggled out of the yellow mac and tossed it up beside the bicycle.

It actually did feel better being out in the rain in just her jeans and T-shirt. Shaking water out of her eyes, Rachel waded forward.

She was in a kind of stream-bed that ran under the road. According to the estate map it was a man-made watercourse, a drainage ditch put in about five years ago.

What was interesting was that there seemed to be clumps of yellow iris along the water's edge for quite a distance—she couldn't see how far in the rain. It wasn't an endangered plant, or even an uncommon one in England, but it was still encouraging to see how quickly adaptation to man's interference had taken place.

'Rachel, what the hell are you doing there?' demanded Grant. As so often with Grant, words were not enough; before she could answer he had plunged down the bank to extract the answer in person.

Rachel didn't look at him. She'd had a lot of practice in not looking at Grant over the past weeks: every time she'd been to the house, in fact. It was embarrassing looking at someone if you'd just been remembering, in lurid detail, every second of the couple of minutes you'd spent in his arms. Since not a day—or, she sometimes thought, an hour—went by without her remembering those two minutes it seemed as if she always *had* been just remembering them every time she happened to come across Grant. If she hadn't, being in the same room with Grant always guaranteed that she made up for lost time.

'Look at this yellow iris,' said Rachel.

'Rachel,' said Grant, 'there is a time and a place for everything, and if you ask me this is emphatically *not* the time to be contemplating the beauties of nature. To mention just one little circumstance, I couldn't help noticing that you're soaked to the skin. It seems churlish to complain when the results are so spectacular—I like to think I have just as much appreciation of natural beauty as the next man, if not more—but you're a valuable commodity, Dr Hawkins, and I don't want you to catch pneumonia.'

'It must have grown up in just five years,' said Rachel.

'You don't say,' said Grant.

'Grant,' Rachel said patiently, 'you don't understand. According to the estate map, this waterway is an extremely recent man-made feature. It's wonderful that such a complex system of waterside vegetation has grown up so quickly.'

Grant squatted down on his haunches just above the waterline and fixed the bed of iris with a thoughtful eye.

'All right, I can see it's nice,' he said. 'But it's still raining, and you're wet, and I'm wet, and staying wet is not going to give it a better chance of survival.' He held out a hand. 'Come on, R. K. V.; we need you back at the ranch.'

His hand grasped hers, and he hauled her out of the water.

'If you want to make yourself useful,' said Rachel acidly, 'you can get the bicycle back on the road. What on earth were you doing out here anyway? Isn't there enough for you to do back at the house? It's a ridiculous time to go careering around the countryside at a hundred miles an hour.'

'I came to pick you up, of course,' said Grant, hoisting the bicycle effortlessly to one shoulder and clambering, not quite so effortlessly, back up the slippery grass bank to the road. 'What happened to you, anyway? Did you lose control?'

'It was deliberate,' said Rachel. 'A four-wheel-drive vehicle was coming the other way at a hundred miles an hour.'

'Completely unnecessary. Look where I stopped,' he said cheerfully, tossing the bicycle into the back. Rachel looked sourly at the vehicle, which stood a good five feet short of the spot where her bicycle track veered suddenly off the road.

'If only I'd known it was you,' said Rachel.

Grant grinned and opened the door for her with a flourish. Rachel climbed in. Grant went round the other side and got behind the wheel.

Suddenly they were cut off from the rain, which now pelted down on the roof of the vehicle. Rachel realised that Grant was almost as wet, though not as dirty, as she was. He was wearing office clothes, though he must have left his jacket in the car when he'd got out; a white shirt was plastered to his muscular chest and shoulders, thin grey trousers clung to sinewy thighs.

'Right,' said Grant. 'First things first. The first thing is to get you out of those wet clothes, and regrettably—' the blue eyes flashed her a gleaming look '—but bearing in mind your value to the project, the second thing is to get you into some dry ones. I think there's a T-shirt in the back. It's not much, but it's better than what you've got on, and we'll be back at the house soon.'

'Good,' said Rachel. 'Then I'll change at the house.'

'You'll change here and like it,' said Grant. He twisted around, extracted a big blue T-shirt and a rather battered pair of khaki shorts from the back, and handed them to her. 'But I promise not to look—at least not for the first thirty seconds.'

'You're just as wet as I am,' said Rachel. 'Why don't you change?'

He grinned at her. 'Only if you promise not to look—the other way, I mean.'

Suddenly, unexpectedly, Rachel found herself laughing. 'You're impossible,' she told him. 'What on earth is the point of getting married if you're going to go on automatically flirting with every other woman you meet?'

'There's nothing automatic about it,' he protested. 'And I don't flirt with *every* other woman—you're the only other woman in my life.'

'And I suppose that makes it a lot better.'

'Of course it does. I think it must be like quitting smoking. You know—you cut down gradually. Well, if I were quitting smoking I'd probably be quite proud of myself for being down to one a day, and I don't flirt with you every day.'

'That's probably because you don't *see* me every day,' said Rachel. 'You flirt with me every time you do see me. I wish you'd stop.'

'I don't see why,' said Grant. 'It can't make any difference to you. You're happily engaged to Mr Clean. You walked away unscathed from a kiss like a charge of dynamite the other day; why should you worry about a little light flirtation?' He was still smiling, his voice light and bantering, but Rachel glanced at him doubtfully.

'You know, I think I got you wrong; you're not Spidergirl at all,' he said. 'You're Supergirl. High explosives go off in your arms without even scorching the costume on the lovely superheroic torso. Speaking of which, if you don't clothe it in that dry T-shirt I'll do it for you with pleasure. It unsettles me to see my pet environmentalist run off the road—I keep forgetting how indestructible you are—and after all the excitement I could do with a cigarette. Aka a little light or not so light flirtation. Tell you what, though—I'll give you sixty seconds.'

He turned abruptly to look out into the rain. 'And one and two and three and four and two and two and three and four and three and two...'

Rachel tore off her clammy T-shirt and put on the dry one in her lap. She pulled off her boots, wriggled out of the cold, wet jeans and slipped into the shorts, which swam on her slim hips. The dry clothes felt very soft and old, wonderfully comfortable after the hard, stiff jeans and chilly shirt she'd taken off. Grant turned back.

'That's better,' he said. 'That's the hell of these environmental impact studies, isn't it? The environment has a nasty habit of making an impact on the student. There's no gratitude in this world.'

'Why do you think I wanted a pink-collar job?' Rachel said bitterly. 'It's all very well for you to go rushing about like a knight in shining armour to rescue me from the elements. If it weren't for you I'd be sitting in a nice dry office telling people you're on another line.'

'You know you love it really,' he told her. He twisted round and now brought a rather battered towel from the back, which was beginning to remind Rachel of the wrecked ship in *The Swiss Family Robinson*. Any minute now he'd bring out a grand piano.

'You don't want to sit around with wet hair,' he informed her, and, before she could stop him, he had thrown the towel over her head and rubbed it briskly over her hair. Somehow, being unable to see made her more conscious of his presence, more aware of the strength and gentleness of the hands that held her head; she could feel her cheeks redden as he pulled the towel away. In spite of herself, in spite of all the arguments she'd had with herself in the last month, Rachel was beginning to be worried. Surely she shouldn't feel this way about another man when she was engaged to Driscoll?

The rain was still drumming on the roof of the four-wheel-drive. Grant ran the towel over his own head, rather less thoroughly than he had over Rachel's, it seemed to her—and after all her hair wasn't any longer than his was. His eyes met hers; the gleam of amusement in them suggested he'd read her thoughts.

Suddenly something occurred to Rachel. Grant thought she'd been unaffected by his kiss, when unfortunately nothing could be further from the truth. Everything he'd said, though, suggested it hadn't just been a casual incident for him either. Maybe it had even had as big an impact on him as it had on her, though that wasn't terribly likely. Yet *he* was obviously still prepared to go ahead with his engagement.

So maybe the fact that she'd thought about it so much was nothing to worry about. After all, Grant had so much more experience than she did. If he could call a kiss 'a charge of dynamite' and see no reason not to marry someone else anyway, there was nothing to worry about. As she looked into that open face, with its amused eyes and faintly smiling mouth, she felt again as she had before, that this was someone she could ask anything.

Fine. She'd ask Grant about it.

'Grant?'

'Yes, Dr Hawkins?'

'I'm not sure "unscathed" is quite the right... I mean, I wouldn't say I was exactly unaffected by that kiss. Do I gather that you—I mean it wasn't just a casual—um—thing for you either?'

'I suppose you do gather that,' he said, still smiling. 'At least, it's one way of putting it.'

'But you're obviously not worried about it; I mean there's no reason as far as you're concerned not to go ahead with your marriage plans. So there's no reason why I shouldn't go ahead with mine.'

'You know what I think of your engagement. Let's not have that argument again,' he said with a shrug.

'But you *would* say it's fairly normal actually to enjoy a little fling with someone else?'

'So it seems,' he said.

'That's what I think too,' said Rachel.

'Are you suggesting we have another one now?' he asked.

Rachel stared at him in dismay. His tone of voice wasn't that of someone trying to trap her or trip her up. It was a simple request for information. The terrible thing was that the idea was suddenly so tempting. Instead of going over and over that same memory she could just kiss him again. It would be wonderful. In fact, it would be better than last time, because this time it could go on a lot longer.

'No,' she forced herself to say. 'I—I don't think that's a very good idea.'

'Neither do I,' said Grant.

He turned round abruptly to bring out—no, it wasn't the Steinway after all—it was the jacket he'd thrown back there when he'd left the car. He put it round her shoulders.

'I think we should get back to the house,' he said.

He turned on the ignition, swivelled so that one arm rested on the back of his seat, and reversed rapidly up the steep slope he'd come down. At the top, he reversed into a small lay-by and turned the vehicle.

The whole thing was done with a kind of careless panache which Rachel found both characteristic and characteristically appealing. Most people would have gone forward half a mile to turn around. Some men would have turned reversing up a hill into a James Bond-type macho display. Grant somehow combined the dazzling technique of Bond with an uncomplicated pleasure in the stunt—why go forward when you had a golden excuse to reverse up a hill at speed? He turned to her now and grinned, and the grin didn't so much say, Aren't I amazing? as, Wasn't that fun?

It occurred to Rachel that Grant was probably the most likeable man she had ever met. Naturally she herself had no desire to spend the rest of her life with a confirmed daredevil; once her contract was satisfied it would be wall-to-wall carpets, nine-to-five office hours and twenty-four-hour-a-day solid comfort for Dr Rachel Katherine Victoria Hawkins. It seemed such a terrible waste, though, that a man who was devastatingly attractive, effortlessly successful and, she would have been willing to bet, the nicest man on the planet should be wasted on a woman who thought a sneer was a waste of good manners on the plebs. If only he could find someone who deserved him!

Rachel sighed.

'Penny for them?' said Grant. They were now bounding over the access road in the other direction.

'I know you don't like me to criticise Olivia,' said Rachel. 'But I just wish you could find someone as nice as you are.'

The four-wheel drive slewed violently to the right, swerved back to the left, narrowly avoiding another ditch, and slowed abruptly to a sedate fifteen miles per hour.

'That's a terrible thing to say,' complained Grant. 'And completely unjustified. But I'm sure you don't really mean it. Just look at you now! You could have spent two months in a comfortable office, which you tell me you prefer, but instead you've spent them roughing it among various bloodthirsty small insects, and all because yours truly demands his pound of flesh. I'm not nice; I'm a ruthless businessman with an engaging smile.'

'So you're well-matched, is that it?' said Rachel snidely.

'I think,' said Grant, and stopped. The four-wheel drive was putt-putting along the track, unaccustomed to this snail-like rate of progress. 'I think most people's marriages are unaccountable to outsiders,' he said at last. 'Maybe it's because you don't just think of the person but of the kind of partnership you're looking for. It's such a permanent thing—it has to do with what you want to do with your life.'

'And you've decided you want to spend yours buying furniture,' said Rachel.

Grant refused to rise to this bait. 'I met Olivia a couple of years ago when I was trying to bring the difficulties of that tribe I told you about to the attention of people who could help. Now, I'd made a lot of people very uncomfortable locally and got a little way just by raising a stink, and if you've got a lot of money you can do some things that otherwise wouldn't be so easy. But basically I wasn't getting very far. Olivia was a big help in getting the right people involved.'

He frowned, hesitating. 'It seemed to me I'd been rather naïve in refusing to have anything to do with the establishment,' he said at last, picking his words carefully. 'They're people, just like everyone else, and if you work with them you can actually get things done instead of wearing yourself out fighting the current.

'I'd had girlfriends before, obviously, but this was the first time I felt of someone that we'd make a good team— that we wouldn't just be idealistic together but do something practical. I'm not saying the personal side isn't there—of course it's there—I'm just saying that it's not the only, or maybe even the main reason for thinking it would be a good marriage.'

'I see,' said Rachel.

She didn't know why this sounded so chilling. After all, it was a version of what she'd said, and believed, of herself and Driscoll. Maybe it was because Grant seemed to be overlooking so much.

'Just be idealistic together'—what would be an ideal world for Olivia? Probably one where she could spend as much money as she liked, Rachel thought cynically. She had seen Olivia fairly frequently in the past few weeks, and it had seemed as though the beautiful blonde girl never talked about anything but how much money the conference centre and science park were likely to bring in.

Once, when writing up her notes, Rachel had overheard a conversation between the engaged couple in the next room—it had begun with wallpaper, so she hadn't felt she should move out of earshot. Then out of the blue Olivia had suggested Grant pay her a salary; he'd asked what figure she had in mind, and Olivia had murmured something.

What value Olivia set on herself Rachel didn't know, but it must have been pretty staggering even for easygoing Grant. He'd given a low whistle; Olivia had pointed out that helping him kept her from taking on other work. There'd been a short pause—then Grant had actually apologised for *taking advantage* of her, and said that if that was the going rate of course he'd pay it! How could he be so blind? It was horrible to hear someone as vital as Grant come up with all these rational arguments for spending his life with someone like that.

'Of course, you're probably thinking that's just the kind of thing you said to me,' said Grant, rather uncannily reading her thoughts. 'But you leave out too much. You're so beautiful and vibrant. I hate to think of you burying yourself alive because of a lot of reasons that sound good in the abstract.'

'*I* leave out too much!' Rachel spluttered. 'At least Driscoll and I are genuinely interested in the same things!' she said, conveniently forgetting how mundane Driscoll's conversation had seemed after Grant's. 'What reason do you have to think Olivia really cares about your project? How do you know she wouldn't have pulled strings for anyone else who could give her the position she wants? I'm sure she's interested in being Lady Mallett when you get that knighthood, and I'm sure she wants to go on going to Paris for her suits, but that's not exactly my idea of idealism. I mean, you could say you share an interest in threatened minorities if you count Paris designers, but I didn't think that was what you had in mind.'

Grant glared at her.

'You hardly know Olivia—' he began.

'Whereas you've made an in-depth study of Driscoll,' Rachel broke in, 'in twenty minutes.'

'We're talking about two different things,' said Grant. 'I wouldn't presume to make pronouncements about what you've got *intellectually* in common with your fiancé; what I said was that the physical chemistry was missing, which any fool could see in two seconds let alone twenty minutes, and that without it there was no point in getting married.

'Now, I certainly don't think you've talked to Olivia enough to know what interests her, and if you think the chemistry is missing bear in mind that we're hardly likely to prove the opposite in the presence of a third party. You may have been misled by the fact that she's not *publicly* demonstrative.'

Rachel tried not to think about Olivia and Grant in private. How dared he be so pompous?

'Well, naturally if you tell me you have a wonderful time in bed I'll take your word for it,' she said tartly. 'But if that's all you've got why get married? You *say* she shares your ideals; what does that mean—she agrees with everything you say?'

'Obviously, since we're in agreement on the important things…'

'What's obvious about it?' asked Rachel. 'It would be more convincing if she *disagreed* with you some of the time. Just think of the way you were in that antique shop— you agreed with everything she said because you didn't care. I'll bet Olivia agrees with absolutely everything you say about the science park, because *she* doesn't care—as long as you get a knighthood and a lot of money, that is.'

Grant's mouth hardened. 'You accuse Olivia of being a snob,' he said, 'but aren't you being one yourself? Olivia hasn't your scientific training; she can't argue about the technical details; you seem to think if someone hasn't got a doctorate she can't care about the future of the planet.'

'That's not fair,' Rachel protested, stung. 'I *didn't* mean that. I just meant that if you cared about furniture you'd have some opinions about it, whether you knew about it or not. If you ask me, *you're* the one who's being condescending,' she added. 'As far as I can see, you don't really care whether she shares your ideals or not—as long as she can pull strings and is good in bed she can think whatever she likes.'

Surprisingly, this gross insult restored him to something like good humour. 'You don't understand,' he said. 'Olivia admits it wasn't something that used to interest her—it was getting involved with me that drew her into it. Obviously I don't expect her to know all about it—it's too new to her to have strong opinions. But the fact that I make allowances for that doesn't mean *my* feelings aren't genuine—just the opposite.'

Rachel realised in despair that it was useless arguing with him. Anyway she didn't know how much more she could stand of hearing about wonderful, sexy, idealistic Olivia.

'Well, I hope you'll be very happy,' she said lugubriously.

'Thanks,' said Grant, and after a short pause added,
'Same here, I'm sure.'

'So why did you come and get me, anyway?' asked Rachel. 'Withdrawal symptoms?'

'I only wish,' said Grant. The four-wheel drive plunged
ahead down the road. 'All hell's broken out. William has
escaped.'

CHAPTER SEVEN

CHAOS and confusion greeted them when the four-wheel drive drew up in front of the house. A little mob of people huddled in the front portico: Grant's new secretary, shuddering convulsively, Olivia, white-lipped, two cleaners exclaiming, 'Horrible, horrible, it was horrible,' and twelve muscular workmen looking uneasily over their shoulders at the door.

'So you're here at last!' exclaimed Olivia angrily, glaring at Rachel. 'I hope you're satisfied!'

'What happened?' asked Rachel.

A chorus of indignant voices broke out in explanation. The gist of this seemed to be that a workman carrying a ladder through the secretary's office had knocked William's glass container to the floor, and it had smashed.

'Oh, my God!' exclaimed Rachel. 'Was he hurt?'

There was another chorus of indignant voices. There was no straight answer to the question, but since he had apparently begun hopping about, 'coming straight at' both the secretary and the workman at the opposite end of the room she hoped that he had escaped unharmed.

Olivia explained coldly that she had come to the door of Grant's office, alarmed by the noise, and had been horrified to see that dangerous spider loose again. She had barely just managed to reach the outer door of the secretary's office, on the heels of the secretary and workman, ahead of the horrible thing, and had had the presence of mind to slam the door shut behind her.

They had put a towel along the base of the door to keep the spider from squeezing out through the millimetre gap between the door and the carpet, it was trapped in the room, and Rachel must instantly get it out.

'All right, all right,' said Rachel wearily. 'But he's really not dangerous, you know. He hasn't got much venom compared to some spiders. He's had a meal recently, so he wouldn't feel like hunting, and he's not naturally aggressive. He was probably more afraid than you were.'

Sixteen sceptical faces met hers. No one said anything, but she got the distinct impression that no one meant to go back in the house, whether or not the office was closed off, until the tarantula was safety back in captivity.

'Come on, Dr Hawkins,' said Grant. 'Spider first, lecture later.'

Rachel stalked into the house. 'Why didn't you just catch him yourself?' she asked.

'Withdrawal symptoms,' said Grant, grinning. 'Actually I wasn't sure if there was a preferred technique for catching them. I remembered you saying they could be quite fragile, and I thought if I accidentally hurt him you'd never speak to me again.'

'Humph,' snorted Rachel. She kicked aside the towel, opened the office door and surveyed the debris inside with a sigh. In their haste to escape, the fugitives had knocked over a table, two chairs and the computer, and papers and wires were everywhere.

'Just close the door again, will you?' she asked. 'And be careful where you step.'

'Yes, ma'am.'

'I'll just poke a few holes in this empty box of photocopying paper, and you can keep him in that until we get another glass case.'

'Oh, I'm still keeping him, am I?'

'Aren't you?' asked Rachel, industriously stabbing the cardboard box with a pair of scissors.

'He seems a little disruptive,' he commented. She could hear the laughter in his voice, and suddenly, as she glanced around, the enormity of what had happened struck her.

This was the office of the head of a multimillion-pound operation. The *computer* had been knocked to the ground, with who knew what irreplaceable materials on its hard disk. Work had ground to a halt throughout the building, when time was of the essence. She'd seen Driscoll speechless with rage when a cup of coffee had been spilt across an easily reproduced paper; how could Grant be so calm?

Come to think of it, he hadn't even seemed particularly concerned to get back when he'd picked her up! How could he waste time telling her to change clothes when his office had been turned upside down?

'I *am* sorry,' she said, suddenly repentant. 'But you know what my aunt's like. Couldn't you keep him in your office, if he bothers your staff?'

'I could,' he admitted. The blue eyes gleamed. 'Do you promise to come and rescue him whenever he gets out?'

'Of course.'

'Then it's a deal.' He stretched out a hand and shook hers solemnly.

'But there's no reason why he should get out.'

'Oh, well, if all else fails I can always leave the top off the case and give him a few torn sheets for a rope-ladder. I get the impression you're avoiding me. Is that because I kissed you?'

'Shouldn't we be looking for William?' asked Rachel.

'I'll promise not to do it again, if you like.'

'Don't be silly.' Rachel flushed.

'You seem strangely impervious to my vivacious charm,' he complained.

'Impossible,' Rachel said sarcastically.

'Well, it's never happened before, but there's a first time for everything.' He grinned at her, and Rachel smiled reluctantly back. 'That's better. Now, do you promise to stop avoiding me?'

'I can't stop something I never started,' said Rachel. 'I wasn't avoiding you. I have work to do. Look, there's William!'

A small black furry leg stepped tentatively out from beneath a half-open catalogue. Slowly, apprehensively, William began to advance across the pale pink wall-to-wall carpet.

Rachel waited. William came closer. Rachel waited. William drew near, in a sudden little jump—and she dropped the cardboard box on top of him. Taking a stiff piece of paper, she slid this under the box and turned the box on its side. She tilted it gradually, and at last rested the box the right way up and placed a lid on it.

'It takes years of training to master this,' she informed Grant drily. 'Good thing you didn't try it yourself.'

He laughed. 'Well, all right, it was an excuse. But if you haven't been avoiding me you've been working too hard. Promise you'll come to the party to celebrate the opening of the conference centre? I don't want to set William loose except as a last resort—I think he finds freedom rather traumatic.'

'All right, you're on,' said Rachel.

'Good. Well, we'd better let everyone back in.' Grant went to the window and shouted to the little group under the portico. 'OK, *coast clear!*'

The workmen dispersed to their duties. The cleaning women said it was time for them to go home, and left, never to return. Olivia returned to the office with Grant's new secretary.

'I'm awfully sorry about the computer, Mr Mallett,' said the secretary, looking at the machine on the floor. 'I was so terrified, I didn't know what I was doing.'

'Oh, that's all right. It can't make much difference now

we're on the network. After all, everything is stored centrally anyway.'

The girl looked uneasy. 'Well—I'm terribly sorry, but for some reason the connection for my computer doesn't seem to have been working terribly well. I know yours got hooked up all right, but I lost a couple of files I tried to save on the network, so I've been saving to my hard disk. The network people are rather hard to get hold of.'

Rachel listened to this in astonishment. The network had been put in place weeks ago, so surely there should have been time to fix any problems? How could you just drift along with a problem like that? Still, presumably the girl had made back-ups of everything on floppy disks.

She glanced at Grant, expecting him to wave aside the accident with his usual friendly offhand manner. His face wore an expression she'd never seen before—no, that wasn't true; she'd seen it just after his interview with Driscoll. Not angry exactly, but the mere absence of its characteristic warmth was startling.

'I see,' he said quietly. 'What a nuisance. Still, I suppose you've got back-ups on floppies?'

'Well, I've got almost everything, but I was only about halfway through that big document you gave me this morning…'

'I see,' he said again. 'In that case it looks as though the first thing is to see if we can get this thing running again, and, if not, see if anything can be salvaged. As you know, we've got a pretty tight deadline on that document. Let me know the state of play in ten minutes or so, will you? Meanwhile I'd better have a word with the network people myself, since it seems they've been giving you a hard time.'

His voice was perfectly level, the words strictly pragmatic—but Rachel thought if she'd been in the girl's place she'd almost have preferred to be shouted at. She felt obscurely embarrassed at being present, but somehow it seemed equally embarrassing to leave. She began, unobtrusively, to pick up papers from the floor.

'That's all right,' said Grant. 'You've been soaked to the skin; you need something to warm you up. Why don't you come into my office? You can have a fortified coffee while I make a couple of calls.'

In the end not only Rachel but Olivia followed him into his office.

'I'm terribly sorry this has happened Grant,' said Rachel as they closed the door on the unfortunate secretary. 'I know it's really all my fault. It would never have happened in the first place if you hadn't taken William.' She wasn't sure she wanted to subject herself to a dose of that chilly rationality, but fair was fair; it wasn't the girl's fault she'd been working in an office with a specimen of wildlife most people found terrifying.

Rather to her surprise, Grant's face lightened. 'Of course it's all your fault,' he agreed as he punched numbers into the phone. 'And mine, for being fool enough to take the damned thing.'

He waited for some time, receiver to his ear, then put it down again. 'No reply,' he said thoughtfully, then shrugged and poured out cups of coffee from a machine in the corner. A bottle of whisky emerged from a cupboard.

'Not for me, Grant,' said Olivia. 'Look, there's something I need to talk to you about...'

Grant added an amount of whisky to Rachel's mug and his own, and passed the mugs round.

'In a moment,' he said. He cocked an eye at Rachel. 'Of course it's your fault, and it's thrown everything in confusion, and it's a nuisance that Jenny's computer may be out of commission. But this has uncovered what seem to be a couple of serious problems. To tell the truth, I'd rather they came to light now than later, when a lot more could stand to be lost than a few hours' copy-typing.'

He took a sip of coffee. 'It worries me that the network

people haven't fixed this problem, whatever it is,' he said. 'It worries me that we can't reach them to get them moving on it. My secretary's way of dealing with the difficulty is obviously a cause for concern. It looks as though we need to get a few things straight, and we may well need to get some new people to take care of our network. That's worth knowing, even at the cost of a little temporary confusion.'

'But Grant,' protested Olivia, 'you can't just take away Xpro's contract just like that. I've known Nigel for yonks. The firm does brilliant work.'

'For other people, maybe.' He shrugged. 'Obviously I'll hear what they have to say first—always supposing I can get through to them.'

'Of course,' said Olivia. 'Anyway, you've only the girl's word for it that the problem really is with the network. If you ask me she's totally incompetent. She was probably doing something wrong and blaming the system.'

Rachel sipped her coffee and sighed, stung for a moment by thoughts of what might have been. She didn't blame Jenny for not having a back-up right up to the last second. She *did* think if she, Rachel, had spent weeks in that deliciously wall-to-wall-carpeted room, instead of up to her thighs communing with the reeds, she would have made Xpro's life miserable until they'd fixed the network, and she'd have kept Grant up-to-date with developments, if only to show her gratitude to the man who'd freed her from the Great Outdoors. Instead the only thing she had to be grateful for was that he'd let her spider come in from the cold.

'Anyway,' said Olivia, after a little pause, when Grant made no response to this remark, 'that wasn't what I had to say to you. I've heard something wonderful! Rupert was staying with Mummy and Daddy last week, and he said Glomac are definitely interested in your science park. They've been looking to build up a base in this area, and he thinks the park would be just the place!'

'Glomac?' said Grant. 'You know what I think about Matheson.'

'I know you had a little disagreement about that drug,' said Olivia. 'I really think you've misjudged Rupert, darling. But anyway, this is something completely different.'

'But they're huge.'

'Exactly. It's a wonderful opportunity!'

'Yes, but we'll only have limited space, after all,' he pointed out. 'The main point is to have a focus for independent researchers and inventors—people who need first-rate facilities but are better off if they can pool some of the resources rather than make a massive capital investment themselves. Glomac would take up an enormous amount of room; in fact they might swallow up the whole shebang. I don't think they're really the kind of outfit we want.'

Olivia stared at him. 'But Grant, you must be sensible,' she said. 'Good heavens, if people hear Glomac want in, the shares will go through the roof. You'd certainly have no problems raising the rest of the finance. You'd have to be mad to turn down something like this.'

Grant smiled at her. 'I know,' he said cheerfully. 'That's what makes it so much fun. I'd love to see the faces on Glomac's board when we turn them down.'

For the second time that afternoon, Rachel felt acutely embarrassed at being where she was. Even the swamp might have been better than this.

It was only too obvious that Olivia was not only not amused but horrified; or rather, it was obvious to Rachel, but Grant seemed so convinced that Olivia shared all his ideals that any other possibility didn't seem to occur to him.

It was equally obvious that Grant had his heart set on a park as he had just described it, and would give up the whole idea sooner than set up operations for a multinational heavyweight like Glomac; or rather, it was obvious to Rachel, but Olivia, for all her dismay at this setback, didn't seem able to believe that anyone could seriously reject the certain prospect of solid cash for what she clearly considered a whim.

'Maybe I'd better be going,' said Rachel.

'But you just got here,' protested Grant. 'And we're having such a lovely time. Tell you what, I'll put this on automatic redial—'

His intercom buzzed. 'Yes?'

The secretary's voice explained, tearfully, that she had been unable to get the computer to start up again. Would Mr Mallett like her to start retyping the material on his computer? She would stay all night to finish it if he wanted her to.

'That's nice of you to offer, Jenny,' said Grant. 'But I think our best bet at this stage is to fax it to the London office. You've got the number of my secretary there? Terrific. Well, give Ellen a call to let her know it's on the way, and ask her to get three or four people working on it up there. There don't seem to be any problems using my computer on the network, so we can print it out down here when it's done.'

Jenny agreed to this. Was there anything else? she asked.

'No, I think that's all. Why don't you give the office a quick tidy and take the rest of the day off? I realise this has been pretty traumatic.'

The intercom crackled in gloomy agreement and fell silent.

'Wonder if I'll see her again?' said Grant. 'Shame she didn't take to William. I suppose I should have introduced them properly when she first came.'

'If you ask me,' said Olivia tartly, 'you should have got rid of that monstrosity weeks ago. For God's sake, Grant, she may not have been very businesslike about back-ups, and she seems to have been hopelessly unprofessional in dealing with her computer, but it's not exactly businesslike of you to keep it here. I trust you're getting rid of it now, anyway.'

'Well, not exactly,' said Grant. 'But I've told Rachel he can stay in my office, so he won't have his feelings hurt by people who don't understand him.'

Olivia gave an impatient little laugh.

'I'm sure that kind of attitude was fine when you were starting out, Grant,' she told him. 'But if you want to accomplish anything you've got to get people to take you seriously. All the more so if you want a—a mixture of smallish businesses in the park, which is bound to make financing more difficult. I know you're used to doing what you like, but you simply can't afford to be so—to be seen as childish.'

Rachel held her breath. She felt as if she'd been watching two cars drive straight at each other at a hundred miles an hour: collision now was surely inevitable? Grant was easygoing, but she was beginning to discover that he had a core of steel. Even the most easygoing of men, anyway, would not take kindly to the implication that the things he cared about most—never mind a stray spider in the office— looked childish.

To her astonishment, Grant threw back his head and laughed.

'My poor darling,' he said, the brilliant blue eyes dancing. 'What a trial I must be to you. Spiders in the office, bats in the belfrey—what have you done to deserve it? Never mind. If we keep quiet about William I think I might just be able to persuade a few people that I'm not a complete lunatic.'

He jumped to his feet, strode across the office, and kissed her quickly. Rather oddly, this seemed to have more of an effect on Rachel than on Olivia. The blonde girl simply stood unresponsively on the spot, and looked up at him with barely concealed impatience when it was over— whereas Rachel felt for a moment as if she'd been kicked in the stomach. Ridiculous. Olivia was his fiancée, for heaven's sake. And it hadn't even been that much of a kiss.

Grant seemed, if anything, rather amused by the lack of response.

'I really do know what I'm doing, you know,' he said, with the kind of smile that always made Rachel's toes curl up inside her shoes. 'But I'm sorry it's so hair-raising for the passengers. Anyway, why don't you show us what you've got lined up for the conference centre? I'm sure that will make people sit up and stare.'

He punched a series of numbers into the phone again, and set it to speaker so that he could dispense with the receiver. He then explained to Rachel that Olivia had taken over the furnishings of the conference centre, since Jenny had felt unable to take on so much responsibility.

Olivia brought out a couple of catalogues and spread them open on the desk. At first reluctantly, but presently with more enthusiasm, she began to outline the equipment she had lined up, while the phone rang and rang at the network support office.

Rachel forced herself to look politely at the catalogues. Grant had put an arm around Olivia's shoulder; Rachel stood on Olivia's other side. She should not be thinking of the hand resting lightly on Olivia's upper arm. She should be concentrating on display boards and overhead projectors. She shouldn't be thinking of the times he'd held her hands, or put a coat round her shoulders, or dried her hair. He was obviously someone to whom physical contact came very naturally; most of the time it didn't mean anything. With his fiancée, obviously, it meant something, and Rachel would do better not to think about it.

She looked down at the glossy pages. Olivia seemed to put a much higher premium on things like presentation binders. Rachel couldn't tell what Grant made of all this; presumably it had his approval.

'Grant told me your suggestion about vending machines,' Olivia remarked, in a bored drawl. 'And I did think about it, but this is such a fabulous old place, isn't it? Obviously one's got to be commercial, but we don't want to be too naff; so I'm afraid I dropped that one.'

Rachel tried to pull herself together. She was engaged to Driscoll. She was being ridiculous. 'It doesn't have to be vending machines, obviously,' she said. 'But scientists and academics don't really care that much about gracious living; they just want to talk, and most of them spend their lives talking over plastic cups of coffee in the basements of libraries and laboratories. A conference gives them the chance to talk to people they won't meet on their home turf.'

Olivia glanced at her, one beautifully groomed eyebrow raised. Rachel was suddenly conscious of the fact that she was wearing a large ancient blue T-shirt that did not belong to her, tattered shorts that obviously didn't belong to her, and a man's jacket that obviously belonged to Grant. As a credible spokesperson for what the high-powered researcher was really looking for, she could probably give Mickey Mouse a run for his money.

'Well, I'll bear that in mind,' said Olivia.

'Yes, see if you can't come up with something that doesn't outrage your sensibilities too much,' said Grant. He gave Rachel a hint of a smile over the lovely blonde head. 'Dr Hawkins is our resident expert, you know. We ignore her advice at our peril.'

Suddenly Rachel had had enough.

'I'd better be going,' she said abruptly. 'It's still only early afternoon, Grant. I'll take the computer into town and see if someone can revive it for you.' She slipped the jacket off her shoulders and draped it over a chair. 'I'll drop these things off here tomorrow.'

'No hurry, but must you go now?' His arm still rested easily round Olivia.

'Yes, I'd better.'

There was a short silence, in which they realised that the

telephone at the network support office was still ringing, and ringing unanswered.

'All right. You can take the four-wheel drive and bring that back tomorrow.' He dug into a pocket, extracted keys, and handed them to her.

The phone was still ringing. Grant looked at it thoughtfully. At last he picked up the receiver and put it down again with a click. His arm slid down from Olivia's shoulder; Rachel felt something strangely like relief.

'Well, darling,' he remarked, still looking at the phone, 'any friend of yours is a friend of mine. I do hope taking our business elsewhere won't spoil the friendship.'

Olivia looked stonily at the phone, and then at Grant's face. Any minute now she would say something cutting, and Grant would laugh again and pull her into his arms.

'I'll bring back the car first thing,' Rachel said hastily, and she almost ran from the room.

CHAPTER EIGHT

RACHEL twisted and turned in front of the mirror for a final inspection. The conference centre had miraculously made its deadline: halfway through May it was actually ready to open. It wasn't strictly necessary, as Olivia had pointed out, for the resident environmentalist to come to the inaugural party, but Grant had quashed this objection without hesitation. It could only do good, he had argued, to have a rising young scientist present. Especially an ornamental one, he had added rashly, and Olivia had abandoned the discussion. In the face of Olivia's scepticism Rachel had determined to do justice to the occasion.

Rachel surveyed herself now with a mixture of pleasure and nervousness. Did she really dare wear this in public?

The dress was black velvet, with a skirt that flared from the narrow waist to just below the knees, and a bodice cut as low as was compatible with being there at all. It made a sort of gesture to modesty—above the velvet filmy black gauze rose to the neck and formed long sleeves to the wrist—but it was still a far cry from the kind of dress worn in academic circles.

Still, at least for once she didn't look like Boy Wonder. Since Driscoll was not going to be there, it was perhaps a little odd that she had gone to so much effort to dazzle, but she was not going to think about that.

She put on dark red lipstick and a dramatic sweep of eyeliner, and surveyed herself again.

Not bad, if she said so herself. Her hair had grown to a

black thatch now, but it still had a gamine quality that contrasted strikingly with the sultry make-up and sexy, sophisticated dress. To look at her, you would never have thought the woman in the mirror had spent half her life counting the movements of small insects in grass habitats, making notes on graph paper and drinking stale water from a plastic flask. Rachel gave herself an approving nod, slipped into filmy tights and very high-heeled black court shoes, and was ready to go.

Olivia was clearly startled, and none too pleased, by her appearance, though after her first double take she did her best to seem noncommittal. Grant was less self-restrained.

'R. K. V.!' he exclaimed, his eyes lighting up as she entered the foyer. 'You look sensational. Try not to let them know you're doing the environmental impact study, though; they won't believe anyone without horn-rimmed glasses can possibly be any good.'

In fact Rachel spent the first half of the evening talking scientific shop with various acquaintances. Professor Edwards, her former supervisor and an eminent zoologist, had come, as had a number of other colleagues. The evening actually demonstrated the excellent adaptation of the building to its new purpose: people were encouraged to wander about exploring the facilities, and those with similar interests rapidly discovered the small nooks which were so convenient for quiet, intense conversation.

'You've done a first-rate job here, Mallett,' said Professor Edwards, drawing Grant into the little circle that already held Rachel and a couple of former fellow research students. 'Trouble with a lot of these places is they're set up by administrators, people who see what a conference is on paper and organise for that.'

He snorted. 'Right, they say, what have we got here? Fifty papers in three days—that's six coffee breaks, two breakfasts, two dinners, three lunches and a hell of a lot of photocopying—and they don't give you a place to go to talk to the person who was your only reason for coming to the damned thing in the first place. So you end up sitting in someone's bedroom or a broom closet, or going down to the local pub.'

'I'm glad you approve,' said Grant.

'Think I'm being polite, don't you? I'm never polite—waste of time. We've already made arrangements for our biennial meeting next spring, more's the pity, but we're having a kind of impromptu conference in September on some very interesting results that have just been published on Madagascar. I'll have a word with the Secretary, tell him to book us in here.'

'That's wonderful news,' said Grant, smiling.

'It's not wonderful,' corrected Professor Edwards. 'It's moderately good news: it's not much of a conference. But if we like what we see we'll be back, and the biennial is the kind of three-ring circus this place is meant for.'

Grant grinned. 'Well, we'll have a glass of champagne anyway, shall we? I'm afraid it's only moderately good champagne, but perhaps you won't mind, in the circumstances.' He strolled off in the direction of the bar.

Rachel smiled in spite of herself. Grant seemed to have got the measure of Professor Edwards in three minutes flat—something some people didn't manage in years.

'I'm sorry Driscoll couldn't be here to see you again,' she said, with an unfortunate association of ideas.

'Humph,' said Professor Edwards unenthusiastically.

'He's been short-listed for the Birmingham job, so he couldn't come,' she explained conscientiously.

Even if Driscoll didn't get the job, which on past performance seemed reasonably likely, it could only do him good for word to get around that he'd been on the short list. Professor Edwards was a notorious gossip, after all. He was exactly the kind of person who could be relied on to pass on the news to other people in the subject—people who could be useful to Driscoll if they remembered his existence and thought of him in connection with things like jobs and, presumably, glowing references.

To her surprise, the professor frowned horribly. 'The Birmingham job? Impossible. You must be thinking of something else. Unless perhaps he was applying to a school?'

'No, I'm sure he wasn't,' insisted Rachel.

'Well, it certainly wasn't the university job,' he said positively. 'There were only four people on the short list, and he wasn't one. I don't even think he was on the long short. Which is hardly surprising, considering...'

'Considering what?' asked Rachel, with a sense of foreboding.

But Grant had returned with the champagne.

'Today Madagascar, tomorrow the world,' he said cheerfully, raising his glass.

Professor Edwards snorted.

Grant laughed. 'I know—conferences are all very well as far as they go, but how far is that? To tell the truth, I'm really expecting more from the science park. We just need planning permission in order to finish raising the capital, so it's a matter of waiting for Rachel to complete her study, and then—well, blast-off into the twenty-first century, but of course I would think that, wouldn't I? Meanwhile we're still waiting to hear whether most resident ants prefer grandchildren or knitting as a leisure interest.'

Edwards pricked up his ears, and asked Rachel a number of questions about the area and the methods she was using, from time to time putting a probing question to Grant about the type of research he expected to be done there. Rachel was kept busy fielding questions, and all the time there was a heavy, leaden feeling in her heart. What could he have meant?

At last Grant went off to join another group and she was able to tax her supervisor again. 'What were you going to say about Driscoll?' she asked tensely.

'Oh—ah—er...' Astonishingly, the bluff man looked

embarrassed. 'I was just wondering whether he'd considered changing career,' he said at last. 'I really don't think much of his chances, Rachel. Now, if it were thirty years ago I don't suppose there'd be a problem, but what with the cuts...' He shook a mane of white hair regretfully. 'Shocking, shocking. Why, I've seen absolutely brilliant young men—and women too, of course—unable to get a job. With that kind of competition, it's simply not realistic to expect people to look at Driscoll.'

'But he's got a terrific publication record!' protested Rachel.

'There's a lot *of* it, certainly, but the problem is, people can read,' Edwards said drily. 'I realise affection has made you partial, but surely you must see he's not in your class? It's not just that there's a world of difference between your solo efforts and his—there's a difference between things he lists that he collaborated on with you and what he did on his own. Funny thing is, to *talk* to him you'd think *he'd* done the bulk of the work on the joint efforts—his ideas, you just helpful.

'Well, as I said, people can read, and they can think too, and they don't much like someone riding on someone else's back. Driscoll really should stop wasting his time and look for some other line of work. You can tell him I said so if you like—more tactfully than I should, I dare say.'

He saw, with relief, that a colleague was trying to attract his attention, and excused himself hastily. Rachel stared unseeingly at the floor, then wandered dully out of the room into the corridor that ran the length of the building. With a vague desire to mull things over on her own, she walked down to the end before opening a door at random. It seemed someone else had had the same idea—a couple were standing by the window, so deep in conversation that they didn't notice the door had opened.

'It's awfully sweet of you, Rupert. I really am a bit

strapped just now.' The voice was Olivia's—Rachel froze on the threshold.

'Don't mention it. You know your father's an old pal of mine. Anyway, I'm counting on you to convince that young hothead of yours that I'm not the monster he imagines.' Matheson laughed indulgently.

'I'm sure he'll come round,' said Olivia.

'I hope he does.' Matheson paused. 'I'm sure it's in his best interests to let us deal with the development of this drug; perhaps you can make him see that. It's the safest way for him to raise money; after all, these environmental impact assessments are very chancy things—you never know what may turn up.'

'I suppose not,' said Olivia.

'And if something turns up and word gets out, it can make investors nervy.' He paused. 'Well, if anything awkward *should* turn up, remember you can always count on me.'

Rachel tiptoed back into the corridor, then walked quickly back the way she had come. She thought Matheson was wasting his time—she'd noticed Grant's look of exasperation when he'd realised that Olivia had invited the man. Still, it wasn't her problem. She had problems of her own.

She crossed the corridor and passed through a bedroom onto a balcony that overlooked the park. The sky was black, the stars brilliant in the country air; the insect sounds of a country night rose from the grounds, and against the black sky she could sometimes see the silhouettes of the tiny bats that lived in one of the towers. At least it was a little better than staying inside making conversation.

Affection makes you partial, Eddie had said. The problem was, it didn't. She and Driscoll had never really bothered with the spontaneous, emotional side of the relationship: whenever she'd tried to build this up he'd accused her of wasting time or destroying his concentration. So she'd just had the idea in her head of a kind of life to-gether—a life which would be based in the scientific world, which in many ways still attracted and interested her, but which would spare her the drudgery she now associated with her area of specialisation.

Now it seemed that it was just an illusion. Without her work and her connections, Driscoll wouldn't have got as far as he had. Trying to go it alone, he'd produced work which she'd always found dull, and now realised was mediocre rather than sound; so he'd used her to get his name on better work, and he'd claimed her ideas as his own, and when even that hadn't worked he'd lied to her about his prospects. So what did that leave?

Well, the problem was that it didn't seem to leave much of anything, but what kind of person did that make you if you dropped someone as soon as you found out he was in trouble? On the other hand, if everything she'd taken for granted about their relationship was wrong, how could she possibly let it go on?

Wearily she leant over the railing and stared out into the night.

Footsteps approached from behind her.

'Rachel? Are you all right?'

'Hello, Grant. Yes, I'm fine. I just came out for some fresh air,' she said, trying to keep her voice steady—but it shook at the end in spite of her.

'Rachel! Someone's upset you! What is it?'

At the sound of his concerned voice Rachel could control herself no longer; she buried her face in her hands and burst into tears.

Suddenly his arm was around her shoulders. 'Rachel! You're crying!' he exclaimed. 'Tell me what it is. Come and sit down over here.'

He led her to a low stone seat which had been cunningly placed so that it was impossible to sit on it and see over the balustrade. Rachel sank onto it, too miserable to resist.

'Now, tell me all about it,' he said. 'And please don't cry. Have a handkerchief. That's better. Now, what's going on?'

'Oh, Grant,' sobbed Rachel, drenching the handkerchief. 'I don't know what to do.'

'Tell me who's upset you and I'll punch his nose,' he offered handsomely.

'You can't do that,' said Rachel, smiling feebly. 'It's Professor Edwards, and he'd take back his Madagascar conference.'

'To hell with his Madagascar conference—'

'And anyway it wasn't his fault; he was just telling the truth.' Haltingly, she repeated what Professor Edwards had said.

'So now I don't know what to do,' she said wretchedly. 'It seems so selfish and disloyal to break up with someone when he can't get a job. But how can I go ahead and marry him just so as not to let him down?'

She turned over the handkerchief, looking for a dry patch, and mopped her eyes with the damp wad.

'I mean, it's not that I mind about the job,' she went on dismally. 'It's not the *job* that matters. After all, if *you* were broke and unemployed you'd still be the same person. But Driscoll hardly seems to exist without somebody's good opinion; when he can't get it from anybody else he has to squeeze it out of me. He tried to cheat other people into thinking well of him by using my work, and he's tried to cheat *me* into thinking well of him by lying to me.'

Grant didn't say anything. His arm was still warm and solid around her shoulders, and he held her close to his side, but he resisted what she supposed must be an overwhelming temptation to say, I told you so.

'And the worst of it is,' she added bitterly, 'that if it hadn't been for him I'd never have done *Son of Thing* after I got that award for *The Thing from the Swamp*.'

'What?' said Grant, startled into speech at last.

'*Aspects of Population Fluctuation in Reedbeds in a Sub-Industrial Environment,*' Rachel said lugubriously. 'Known as *The Thing from the Swamp* to its friends—or should I say enemies?—and closely followed by the rip-roaring read, *Further Aspects of Population Fluctuation in* et cetera, et cetera, et cetera, alias *Son of Thing*. Not to mention,' she continued gloomily, '*Effects on Pampas Populations of Proto-Industrial Development*, aka *Thing Meets Godzilla*. If it hadn't been for Driscoll I could have been studying zebras.'

'You shock me inexpressibly, Dr Hawkins,' said Grant. 'I've read all those studies, at least the published versions, and I thought they were terrific. I'm sorry if you weren't having fun, but your loss is the world's gain. It seems unsporting to kick a man when he's down, so I suppose I can't say what I really think of your soon-to-be-ex-fiancé-if-you've-got-any-sense, but if it was his influence that kept you going it's the first evidence I've seen that he's made a solid contribution to science.'

'That's easy for you to say,' said Rachel. 'You didn't have your body made into a movable feast for mosquitoes. If somebody wants to give a body to science that's fine by me, but he should at least make sure it's his own.'

'That's the spirit,' said Grant. 'Never say die.'

He took her hand in his, stroking the palm gently with his thumb. After a moment's hesitation, he said, 'I'm trying to think of a way of saying this that won't sound like I told you so, but since I can't all I'll say is I think it would have been better if you'd found out sooner, but better late than never. You've already admitted you agreed to leave the physical side of your relationship on the back burner because you shared intellectual goals that you thought more important. Now you find that shared interest wasn't what you thought either.

'By the sound of it, he may actually have used the fact that you were away so much to encourage false ideas of

CHAPTER NINE

RACHEL knew she shouldn't enjoy this. In the first place, Grant was only doing it out of pity. In the second place, he was engaged to someone else. She didn't care. She was being kissed by the man she loved, she was in his arms for the last time in her life, and she intended to make the most of it.

As for Olivia—well, she would be able to kiss Grant morning, noon and night. If Rachel had been in her position it was certainly how she would have spent most of her time—no wonder Driscoll had worried about sex interfering with work. Surely Olivia could spare Rachel just one, from a man who didn't mean anything by it anyway, when she had such orgies in store?

His mouth was soft, gentling hers, the touch almost as light as breath. Her mouth opened; memory hadn't exaggerated either the electric shock of the first contact or the wonderful honeyed taste of his mouth. It also hadn't overstated his technique, which managed to make sheer outrageous virtuosity seductive in itself; in fact it was obvious he hadn't even begun to exhaust his repertoire. His tongue traced the line of her lips, the tip just pressing inside, and she closed her mouth again to hold it tightly between her lips, forcing him to push harder against her resistance.

He laughed deep in his throat, sliding the supple tip with delicious slowness along her tightly closed lips, then forcing it deeper into her mouth, but still slowly, lingering with obvious pleasure to drag out the sensation, the struggle against the pressure of her lips giving way to free movement within. She softened her mouth again against his, and now her tongue moved along his, imitating every tantalising movement with the same lingering delight.

Rachel's head was reeling. Her mouth seemed to melt around his tongue, her knees turned to jelly; she had to hold him now for support. It was wonderful—of course it was wonderful. As good—no, better than she'd remembered. But in a remote corner of her mind she wondered whether she had been insane to invite this.

She realised now that she'd never really desired Driscoll; she'd just assumed that would come when the time came, and she hadn't worried too much when the time kept being put off. Now she seemed to have released a force that was beyond her control; each exquisite sensation left her hungry for more, and her whole body ached with a terrible, unappeasable longing.

She wanted only to hold him closer, to kiss him fiercely until he was as much on fire as she was, to tear his shirt off, or perhaps torment him by undoing the buttons one by one until he, too, lost control and pushed things to their inevitable conclusion.

Except that it wasn't inevitable at all; even as his mouth caressed hers with inexpressible sweetness, she remembered, chillingly, how he had broken off last time when their kiss had become more passionate. She had probably pushed things already, making the kiss more sexual than he had really had in mind. If she put her hands inside his jacket to feel the hard, muscular back, or, worse yet, raised them to his collar to unfasten the button and kiss the soft hollow at the base of his throat, or, for that matter, did any of a number of things that she would once have considered unthinkable, he would step away at once and that would be that.

She knew he had a soft spot for her; that was why he was doing something he knew he shouldn't. There was no way he would let it go any further, though, and if she didn't want him to remember that he shouldn't even be kissing her she had better watch her step. Though every particle of her being ached to hold him closer she forced herself to stand just as she was. She ached to devour his mouth with hard, hungry kisses, but instead she forced herself to soften her mouth again, to keep it as nearly passive as was possible when she was tempted by kisses of such powerful sweetness.

He raised his mouth, and for one terrible instant she thought he meant to stop. His eyes glittered in the dark hollows beneath his brows. 'Rachel,' he said, in a low, hoarse voice. 'My God, you're beautiful.'

He raised one hand to her face and traced, with his index finger, the full, sensitive lower lip, then kissed her lightly again. He raised his head again, a fraction of an inch; she could still feel his breath on her mouth. Rachel held her breath. And then his lips brushed the line of her jaw, and found the delicate skin beneath her ear, and kissed her there until she could feel her pulse hammering under the feather-light touch of his mouth.

Rachel felt as if the slightest breath would break the spell. She stood absolutely still. Now his mouth grazed her throat; now it lingered on the filmy gauze which covered her shoulders. Her eyes closed. Her entire being seemed concentrated on a single, almost imperceptible sensation: the movement of his mouth, as light as a butterfly's wing, down her gauzy sleeve to her wrist. He paused, and kissed the pulse point of her wrist. He kissed the palm of her hand.

Rachel drew in a sharp breath. Her eyes opened. At the sight of his gleaming blond head bent over her hand, the exquisite sweetness of his mouth on the sensitive skin, she felt an almost unbearable stab of desire. 'Oh...' she breathed. She had to force herself not to beg, Oh, *please*.

Suddenly Grant raised his head, letting her hand fall to her side.

All the laughter had vanished from his face. His eyes met hers steadily; his mouth was perfectly serious, with no sign of its characteristic lurking smile.

'I must be insane,' he said. 'This has got to stop.'

'What do you mean?' said Rachel.

'You know what I mean. It's not a— I've tried treating it as a joke, but it's not a joke.'

Rachel gave a rather unsteady smile and shook her head.

'And when you look at me like that—' He made an impatient movement and turned abruptly, gripping the balustrade with both hands and looking resolutely away from her out into the night. He was silent for some time.

At last he turned back. For the first time Rachel was conscious of the nearly ten years' difference in their ages; he looked, she supposed, what he was—a man in the prime of life with all the authority of someone who had built up from scratch, and now ran, a multimillion-pound company.

He looked, for once, the way those people always did in the pages of the *Financial Times*: as though success closed off all but a very few doors, those few being the ones that led to greater success for a multimillion-pound company. Though it was the look of a successful man, it tore her heart to see it. She felt as though she'd somehow made Grant—who always did precisely what he wanted, however insane—see the need to act sensibly.

'You know, you're not at all my idea of a *femme fatale*,' he told her, with a rather strained version of his old smile. 'I think I've always had a mental image of someone with a lot of mascara and a cigarette-holder. That must be why I didn't realise what hit me when I got knocked over by a girl in a Spiderman T-shirt.'

There was no mistaking the implication of this, but it was so wildly improbable that Rachel could only stare at him, her eyes enormous under the fly-away brows.

'I thought you were breathtakingly beautiful the moment I saw you, of course. Somehow it was all the more devastating because you seemed completely unaware of it, wearing that crazy T-shirt and the DMs and carting William around in a box like a boy with a prize beetle.

'Then it turned out I didn't know the half of it. It's not that it doesn't matter what you wear—each time you wear something new it's as if you've found some new, completely different way to be beautiful. But somehow you didn't seem—dangerous. *You* were always the same—funny and clever and set on getting your way; I've never met anyone so easy to talk to.'

'I thought you were like that with everyone,' said Rachel.

'I probably am, but more so with you, if that makes sense.' He looked at her steadily again, with that same terrible air of responsibility. 'The thing is, we've all heard the clichés about men about to get married. You know—however much a man wants to do it, he starts to feel claustrophobic. Suddenly he meets some girl and becomes obsessed. Maybe *she*'s really the one. Maybe he's about to make the mistake of his life. Well, I was convinced—*am* convinced—that marrying Olivia is the right thing to do.'

Rachel shivered. She supposed she should say something sympathetic or encouraging, but she couldn't force herself to utter a syllable.

'So when I met you I thought I'd just fallen victim to the usual syndrome. And it seemed to me that if I resisted it, and avoided you at all costs, I'd just make it worse. I'd build up some image of you in my head, and for the rest of my life I'd go around *wondering*... Whereas if I got to know you I'd get used to you, and the glamour would wear off; or at least, if I didn't pretend I wasn't attracted to you but just treated it as a joke, it would be under control.'

'And wasn't it?' asked Rachel.

'What do you think?' He raised an eyebrow. 'That first kiss should have put me on guard, but—I don't know, you were so positive that it could be put in perspective, and anyway it seemed absurd to blow up a single incident like that out of all proportion...'

He gave a reluctant smile. 'Well, I kept rerunning it on instant replay—so much for not getting obsessed—but I somehow managed to persuade myself that was all part of the joke, having a memory of a kiss like your favourite Test Series highlight. Only, time went on, and every time I saw you I wanted to kiss you again—it was getting to be less and less of a joke. And tonight—well, God knows, you looked miserable and I wanted to make you feel better, but I think as much as anything I hoped that if I stopped thinking about it and just did it I'd get you out of my system. Well, it's fairly obvious now that that's never going to work.'

Rachel didn't know whether it would be worse to agree or disagree with this remark. Considering that she'd just realised that this was the man she loved, and that he now seemed to be saying he found her irresistible, she was surprised by just how nervous all these remarks were making her.

'I think we both know what will happen if we go on in this way,' he told her. 'And I think we both know that we'd be good together. More than good. But I'm not going to start an affair three months before my wedding. Olivia is the right wife for me. I have tremendous respect for her; she'll be a wonderful hostess, and we'll do a terrific job together, and—'

For the first time since she'd known him Grant really did look like a granite-jawed tycoon: there was a hard set to his jaw, a flinty look in the usually dancing eyes. Here was a man who could surmount insurmountable obstacles to reach his goal, and if they included marrying a wonderful hostess, so be it.

Rachel frowned. She supposed she should feel crushed. It was not humanly possible to feel miserable, though, when the man you loved had just said you were breathtakingly beautiful, beautiful, funny, clever, easy to talk to and beautiful. He couldn't say enough about how wonderful she was; the contrast with his efforts to find a good word to say for Olivia was almost ludicrous.

It would have been funny if he hadn't been planning to marry her in three months. Three months! Even unconventional Grant would probably shrink from backing out once the invitations had been sent and a wedding list started at Harrods. Wasn't there any way out?

It wasn't just a question of compliments. Rachel had stared despondently at her funny face too often not to have a pretty fair idea of its merits. A man who thought she was breathtakingly beautiful had to be either mad...or madly in love.

Besides, hadn't she herself spent months trying to remind herself of Driscoll's good qualities, in the face of Grant's wit, charm, intelligence and overwhelming physical attractiveness? She knew, only too well, how easy it was to talk yourself out of seeing the obvious. But would Grant recognise that in time?

'Are you planning to have children?' she asked abruptly, trying unsuccessfully to imagine Olivia as a mother. She could imagine Grant as a father, all right—or, at least, she could imagine the Grant of the past few months in that role, though quite what the steely-eyed man beside her would make of it was another matter.

'Of course,' said Grant. 'That is, we haven't discussed it, but obviously...'

'Well, it may be obvious to you,' said Rachel. 'But it might be a good idea to make sure it's obvious to her before the ceremony. You don't want any nasty surprises on your wedding night.'

'Of course,' Grant said stiffly. 'The point I'm trying to make is that I think you and I should have a more formal relationship in future. I don't want to hurt your feelings— it's nothing against you personally; in fact I've never met a woman I liked so much——but I think it would be better if I kept you at arm's length.'

'I don't think there's anything very formal about putting your hands on my shoulders,' Rachel said pertly. 'I suppose it might help if you called me Dr Hawkins.'

'You know perfectly well what I mean,' said Grant.

'Would you like me to call you Mr Mallett?' she asked helpfully. Clever, funny, determined to get her way——that was what he'd said he *liked* about her. So if she said what naturally came to mind he'd be amused.

The old Grant would have been amused. Mr Gimlet-Eye was not so easily entertained.

'That won't be necessary,' he said drily.

'Shall I promise to keep you at arm's length?' she asked, raising one of her elfin eyebrows. She laid one of her arms, in its filmy gauze sleeve, along the length of his, resting her hand on his shoulder, and looked up at him quizzically.

Grant took her hand in his free hand, took it off his shoulder and dropped it. 'We both know what the situation is,' he said even more drily. 'There's a very strong physical attraction between us; but the kind of——flirtatious friendship we've had is just as dangerous. I thought we could discuss this like adults. It seems I was mistaken.'

Looking on the bright side, at least she hadn't said that if he ever wanted to have another try at getting it out of his system he knew where to come. Something told her that would not have been well received.

His expression was stern, almost forbidding. In fact, she realised rather helplessly, she had no idea what to say to this grim individual. Reason protested that he was simply trying to make a virtue out of undergoing a lifetime of unnecessary unpleasantness, but reason didn't allow for how daunting he could be when he set aside his usual easygoing manner and revealed the formidable will-power beneath.

'I don't think we have anything else to say to each other,' he said. 'I hope you find what you're looking for.' And without another word he walked off down the balcony, his heels ringing out on the tiles.

CHAPTER TEN

AFTER going through this emotional wringer, it came as a surprise to Rachel to remember that she was actually still engaged to Driscoll. Somehow the decision to end that already seemed so obvious, so remote, that it seemed astonishing that the necessary action hadn't already taken place.

She knew she should be trying to think of the right way to break the news; instead, she found herself going over and over everything Grant had said. 'Breathtakingly beautiful' was still her favourite phrase, though she also liked the part about finding some completely new way to be beautiful every time he saw her—but unfortunately the horrible, cold tone of his voice at the end kept coming back to haunt her. There had been something close to contempt in his voice at the end, as if Grant, who'd always preferred a light touch, had suddenly decided it was frivolous.

She tried to tell herself that it didn't mean anything, that he was trying to force himself to do something against his will, but it was impossible to hear that terrible tone of voice from the man you loved and just shrug it off. Whenever she did manage not to think of it, the most terrible words of all came to torment her: 'Three months before my wedding.'

She had been agonising over this all night when Driscoll called the next morning.

'How—how are you?' she asked. She couldn't bring herself to ask the question that would have been natural in the circumstances, to ask how the interview had gone when she knew he hadn't had one.

'Terrible,' said Driscoll. 'I think this has been a waste of time, to tell the truth. Apparently Ferguson is the inside candidate; the interviews are just a matter of going through the motions.'

'I'm sorry to hear that,' said Rachel.

'You haven't happened to hear whether they'll be needing someone again next year to teach the freshers?'

'N-no, I'm afraid I haven't.'

'You really should make more of an effort to keep your finger on the pulse, Rache,' said Driscoll. 'I hope you see now how disastrous it was taking those six months off. You seem to be completely out of touch these days.'

'Could be,' said Rachel.

Her tone lacked the warm sympathy which usually greeted Driscoll's set-backs. 'Is there something wrong?'

Rachel had meant to wait until they were together again, but suddenly she couldn't face the alternative—a conversation in which she pretended everything was fine, perhaps even expressed sympathy over an interview she knew hadn't taken place.

'It's just—I don't think this is working out, Driscoll,' she said in a rush. 'We've tried to make it work, but I don't think this is right for me.'

The next ten minutes were horrible. Driscoll at first couldn't understand, then refused to believe she was serious. Worst of all, he sounded genuinely aggrieved that she had been so inconsiderate as to bring this up when he'd just had a terrible interview—even though the interview was one he'd made up.

Rachel argued drearily on, hampered by the fact that the one thing that might have convinced him—that she'd fallen in love with someone else—was the one thing she had to deny flat out. The only person she'd had the opportunity to meet for weeks was Grant. She shuddered to think what might happen if news got around that she'd fallen for him, especially now that Grant was so determined to behave like an adult. At last Driscoll ended the conversation, stating his intention of coming to see her as soon as his other commitments allowed.

For once Rachel was actually glad to spend her time outside doing her fieldwork. The recording of detailed observations forced her to concentrate, forced her to stop thinking constantly about Grant, and occasionally about Driscoll.

A week went by in which, surprisingly, she heard nothing from Driscoll. She also didn't see much of Grant, who was spending a lot of time in his London office. She did see rather a lot of Olivia, who was finalising decoration of the private parts of the mansion.

Rachel kept her records in an office at Arrowmead. On average an hour of observation generated two to three hours' work in the office identifying insects and unfamiliar plants before the final account of the day's work could be written up. She kept hoping Grant would be there, but it seemed as though she was always running into the beautiful blonde girl instead.

Olivia was always beautifully groomed, while Rachel was usually knee-high in mud. Rachel knew which of the two *she'd* be impressed by if she were thinking of investing a couple of million or so. In spite of herself, she began to have doubts.

Maybe Grant *had* made the right choice. Maybe it was all for the best.

She was debating this for the fiftieth time when she bicycled up to the house one evening for William's weekly feeding. Grant was supposed to be back today, she remembered. He must have a huge amount to catch up on; he'd probably be in his office.

Well, she resolved virtuously, she'd just have to try not to disturb him. Her mouth curved involuntarily as various enjoyable ways of disturbing Mr Mallett came to mind. She would be very, very good, she told herself, pedalling faster.

Considering that she'd promised herself not to disturb Grant, it was unreasonable to mind that it was unexpectedly hard to get the chance. Rachel knew she was being unreasonable, but she still glared at Driscoll, unexpectedly discovered reading in Reception, the way some women glared at spiders.

'What are you doing here?' she asked impatiently.

'I came to find you,' he said simply.

His black hair was tidy, the horn-rimmed glasses severe. He looked reprovingly at Rachel through the glasses, with the air of Scientific Man gazing at Irrational Female.

'You seemed a little overwrought when we spoke,' he said. 'Your aunt and uncle said you often didn't get back until late. I thought it might be helpful, too, if I had a look at your results. So I came over here.'

Rachel didn't much want a private talk with Driscoll, but it was better than one with an audience.

'My results are just down the corridor,' she said reluctantly. What if Grant had left by the time she'd finished with Driscoll? Well, she thought gloomily, best to get this over with. She led Driscoll to her tiny office.

The discussion was as bad as she'd feared. Driscoll was at first sceptical, then impatient, and at last bitterly reproachful.

'You don't seem to understand how much I've invested in our scientific partnership,' he complained. 'It's practically impossible to say who did what work. Now I'll have to stake out a completely new territory. You know what the job climate is like these days. That's a luxury I really can't afford.'

Rachel thought she wouldn't have had too much trouble working out who should get the credit for what, but she did feel sorry for Driscoll. Some magical instinct for self-preservation kept her, however, from agreeing to his suggestion that he help out on the current project as a stopgap measure.

Unfortunately the instinct must have then decided it had done a day's work. It occurred to Rachel that she really ought to pass on Professor Edwards' advice; no sense of self-preservation suggested that this was really not the time.

'Have you ever thought of leaving academia?' she asked tentatively.

She had no opportunity to say anything else for quite a long time. Driscoll had *not* thought of leaving academia.

'How can you be so unbelievably inconsiderate as to suggest that at a time like this?' he demanded. 'How can you be so childish? I suppose,' he went on, with a belated attempt at dignity, 'that the profession has room enough for the two of us. I suppose we can behave like adults. I need hardly add,' he added, 'that I still feel considerable interest in your work here, and would appreciate the opportunity to examine your results.' The horn-rimmed glasses dared her to object.

Rachel wished people would stop going on about behaving like adults. What it seemed to mean was politely doing something insane. She didn't have the heart to argue the point with Driscoll, though. She just hoped he'd be adult enough not to spill ink all over her work.

'Of course you're welcome to look at it,' she said. 'Do you mind if I leave you to it, though? I've got something to discuss with Mr Mallett.'

That was a nice grown-up way of referring to feeding time for William. Something told her it would carry weight with Driscoll.

'Don't let me stop you,' he said peevishly.

'I'll look back in on you in a bit,' Rachel promised. If that wasn't insane politeness at its adult best, what was? Meanwhile she had a hungry tarantula to think about.

She left the room and headed for Grant's office with a light step. She wouldn't *disturb* him, of course, but naturally they would get into conversation while she fed William. Rachel couldn't help feeling she deserved a little light relief after all this talk with Driscoll.

If only Grant was still there! It was true that he'd said they should be more formal, but Grant didn't have a formal bone in his body. He'd just been feeling depressed by his engagement, she decided. Maybe he'd have started to see reason by now. Even if he hadn't, though, she could do with some light-hearted banter after an hour or so of gloom.

'Does Grant have anybody with him?' she asked the secretary.

'No, but he's pretty busy—' The girl broke off as the intercom crackled.

'Isn't that draft prospectus ready yet?' snapped an impatient voice.

'I'm afraid not; it may be another half an hour—'

'You do understand that this is extremely urgent?'

'I've had a lot of interruptions this afternoon,' the girl said apologetically.

'Well, get a move on, will you?'

Rachel decided that maybe she wasn't the stuff perfect secretaries were made of after all. She couldn't imagine putting up with that nonsense for more than two seconds. It didn't take much to work out who'd been doing the interrupting.

'I won't disturb him,' she assured the secretary.

'I think that's probably best,' admitted the girl, looking relieved.

It was only when Rachel headed for the door of Grant's office that the misunderstanding became clear—and then it was too late.

'Hello,' said Rachel cheerily, closing the door smartly behind her. 'Bad day?'

Grant looked up from some papers and frowned at her. He looked at least as severe as Driscoll, and a lot more formidable. 'What are you doing here?' he asked.

'I won't disturb you,' Rachel promised him.

'You are disturbing me.' Once it would have been a compliment; now he just sounded annoyed. 'What are you doing here?'

Rachel would not have liked this tone of voice from anyone. She would have liked it even less from a man she was in love with, whatever their relations had been. Hearing it from Grant, though, made her feel she might go off like a firecracker.

This was a man who'd flirted with her unmercifully for the first three months of their acquaintance. He'd kissed her twice and danced with her once, and he had *insisted* on keeping William in his own office because, if you please, he didn't want Rachel to avoid him. He'd insisted on taking William in the first place, in fact, purely to annoy Driscoll. And now listen to him!

'I've come to feed William,' Rachel said coldly. 'Just because you don't want to flirt any more it doesn't mean William can miraculously feed on air.'

'All right, get on with it, then.'

'Yes, *sir*!' said Rachel, saluting smartly.

She ambled, as slowly as she dared, to the filing cabinet on which William's new glass box had been placed. It was a way of walking which did a lot to emphasise the shapely curve of her hips and her spectacular long legs in their skin-tight, ancient jeans.

It seemed to do nothing to improve Grant's temper, though; she could see his lips tighten. What a shame!

Rachel hopped up onto the filing cabinet beside William and opened her little plastic box of goodies.

'Maybe it's a good thing I didn't become your secretary after all,' she remarked, tossing William an appetiser. 'Are you like this all the time now?'

'Like what?' he asked through gritted teeth. For all his impatience he hadn't made much of an effort to go back to his papers, she noticed; was that a good sign?

'Impatient and bad-tempered,' Rachel replied promptly.

'I've got an important deadline coming up, if that's what you mean,' he said, scowling.

Driscoll only looked sulky when he scowled; Grant looked much more forbidding. All the more reason not to be daunted, she told herself.

'Do important deadlines always make you pompous and irritable?' she asked sympathetically. 'It must be a terrible nuisance.' She dropped a couple of small snacks over the side of the glass.

Suddenly Grant stood up, pushing back his chair. He walked towards her across the carpet with a steady, measured stride very different from her own hip-swinging progress earlier; well, she supposed this was what she'd wanted. He stopped and looked at her thoughtfully, the brilliant blue eyes on a level with hers.

'Rachel,' he said very quietly, 'do you have any idea what it takes to get something like this off the ground?'

'What do you mean?' asked Rachel.

'You've got to persuade investors that you can attract first-class people, and at the same time persuade first-class people that you'll be able to offer the facilities that will make it worth their while to make a definite commitment—everyone wants someone else to make an ironclad commitment first. It takes a lot of time, and a lot of money—money that's a dead loss if nobody bites.'

It was hard for Rachel to imagine anyone not instantly agreeing to anything Grant suggested. 'I can see it must be difficult,' she said.

'That's one word for it,' he said. 'But it's worth it—you of all people should see that. You must at least have some idea of the kind of difference the place could make if it worked.'

'Yes,' said Rachel. She wondered for a moment whether she dared to say what she wanted to say. Probably not. 'But I don't think any of those risks would bother you if you weren't making the ultimate sacrifice,' she said, saying it anyway.

The blue eyes blazed with anger. Rachel pressed on regardless.

'You're sacrificing your own happiness for the cause,' she added unrepentantly. 'So you think that gives you the right to make everyone else unhappy as well.'

'I'm not unhappy,' he told her grimly. 'My life is exactly the way I want it.'

'Of course you're not happy!' Rachel threw caution to the winds. 'I know what you're going through, Grant, and you just can't do it! I've just broken off with Driscoll—'

'Congratulations.'

'—and it's like being let out of prison. You were absolutely right,' she said urgently. 'I tried to ignore it, but I couldn't. But don't you see? I do know what you're going through. You can't possibly keep it up, Grant. You've got to end it now, before it's too late!'

'I think you're getting a bit carried away, Rachel,' he said quietly. 'I'm glad you've put an end to your engagement, since he obviously wasn't in your league. Our cases bear no comparison, however.' His voice was even. 'As far as I can make out, you'd never been seriously involved with anyone before you entered into this relationship. By your age I'd already had plenty of experience, and it's been a while since I was your age. I know what I'm like, and what I'm looking for. I'm perfectly capable of choosing the right partner for myself.'

Rachel tried to rally under this comprehensive snub. He was getting as pompous as Driscoll, she told herself. The problem was, though, that when Grant decided to pull rank he was overwhelming. He looked worldly and experienced; he made her feel silly and callow. Even worse, he'd retreated behind an armour of self-certainty which seemed well-nigh impenetrable. She had to remind herself that she *knew* he'd talked himself into this. She knew, too, only too well, that there was an infallible way of getting not only behind the armour but under his skin—*if* she had the nerve to use it.

'I see,' said Rachel. 'I thought the main evidence of my inexperience was the fact that I hadn't realised I'd be frustrated. Now it seems it's all your experience which enables you to decide you don't mind.'

'I'm perfectly happy—'

'How can you be happy if you're frustrated?'

'I am not frustrated,' he snapped.

'So this doesn't do anything for you?' asked Rachel. She wasn't going to kiss him—at least, not just yet—but she put out a hand to his jaw and ran her thumb over his lower lip.

He stepped back abruptly. His face was thunderous. 'I don't have time to waste on this,' he said.

If she hadn't actually had the proof before her eyes, Rachel wouldn't have believed that someone with Grant's debonair good looks could appear so deadly. His eyes had not only the colour but the hardness of sapphires; his jaw was hard, his mouth not only hard but ruthless.

'If you have to disturb me to feed the spider, you'll have to take him with you now,' he said coldly. 'If you can't take him away, I want him fed before seven in the morning. I don't want you in my office when I'm working unless you have a problem with the environmental assessment that requires my personal intervention. Is that understood?'

Rachel told herself she knew why he was being so horrible, but it didn't help. She couldn't help shrivelling up inside under that angry, contemptuous look.

'Yes,' she said.

'Have you finished feeding him now?'

'Yes,' she admitted.

'Then perhaps you'd be good enough to leave,' he said crisply.

Rachel slunk out of the room.

CHAPTER ELEVEN

AFTER that disastrous interview the last thing Rachel wanted was to talk to Driscoll. Still, she could hardly just walk out without saying goodbye. Reluctantly she returned to her little office.

To her surprise she found Driscoll deep in conversation with Olivia.

'So it's really not possible to plant some rare species here?' Olivia was saying.

'Well, it would depend on the species—part of the problem is getting the plants, of course. If they're rare they're usually protected, so one couldn't just go digging them up—at least not in broad daylight.' Driscoll gave a rather sly laugh.

Olivia caught sight of Rachel. 'Your friend has been setting my mind at rest,' she said. 'So much is riding on this environmental impact study—what's to stop one of Grant's enemies from just planting rare species here and sabotaging it? But Driscoll tells me the plants couldn't transfer that easily.'

'And even if they could be transplanted it would be hard to find plants that would be convincing in the context,' Rachel reassured her. 'Rare species don't exist in isolation; each one is embedded in a whole habitat—and you couldn't very well transfer *that*. If something didn't belong I'd probably be able to get to the bottom of it long before we actually submitted the report and the application for planning approval.'

'I see.' Olivia looked thoughtful. 'Well, I'd still like this place to be a haven for ecologically threatened plants if we can get some. I know it's what Grant would want.' She smiled at Driscoll, who smiled back, dazzled. 'I understand your friend here is between jobs; I'd like him to look into it for me and see what we can do. Obviously we'd expect to pay well for someone with such a high level of expertise.'

'It's wonderful to meet a member of the general public with an appreciation of the importance of this work,' said Driscoll, brightening at the mention of money.

Olivia sighed and shook her head. 'It's tragic the way some of the best people get passed over in academia,' she said. 'I think you'll find industry is a different story. I realise this can only be a short-term proposition for someone with your background, but I'll certainly have a word with Rupert Matheson.'

'The head of Glomac?' Driscoll said incredulously.

'He's a good family friend. I'm sure he can find something for you. A man in his position knows that first-rate people sometimes don't do as well in interviews as flashier, superficial people—I know you'll be a tremendous help to me, and I'll make sure Rupert knows you're the kind of man he's looking for.'

Driscoll flashed a triumphant glance at Rachel before stammering his thanks.

'I know you and Driscoll have had a little tiff,' Olivia added suavely. 'But I'm sure we can all behave like adults, can't we?'

Rachel tried to muster her last drop of adult politeness. She agreed to this and excused herself politely. Now that her office had been taken over she couldn't work anyway, she told herself; she might as well go home.

She bicycled gloomily off down the drive. For a minute or so she wondered idly why Olivia should want to flatter Driscoll, or hire him, or help him—she didn't seem the altruistic type. But then she remembered Grant, and had no attention to spare for trifles like the strange conversation she'd just heard.

Rachel did not have another chance to talk to Grant at length. Occasionally she ran into him when she went back to the house to deal with her records; he was always meticulously polite and repellingly formal. He always seemed to be frowning now, and hardly seemed to speak except to bark orders.

Rachel tried to tell herself it was just because he was unhappy, but that didn't make it any easier to take. He'd obviously made his choice, and nothing as lightweight as her inexperienced self could talk him out of it. Too right she wasn't a *femme fatale*, she thought gloomily; any *femme fatale* worth her salt would have had him at her feet. Instead, she'd simply driven him further into this new mania for work.

Well, it was probably all for the best, she assured herself, after another two weeks of the cold shoulder. She scowled up at the gathering clouds above the reedbed. Drops of rain splashed on the water; the wind was beginning to rise.

Did she want to be here? She did not. Whose fault was it that she was standing here? Grant Mallett's. Any man with a scrap of decency would have released her from her contract and let her move into a comfortable office; Grant had insisted she finish the work, because, obviously, he hadn't a scrap of decency and was a selfish swine. Did she want to marry a selfish swine? No. Well, yes, but that was a temporary lapse of sanity; she wasn't *going* to marry a selfish swine, and it was all for the best.

Lightning flashed on the horizon. Hastily Rachel dictated a few more remarks into her tiny tape recorder and tucked it safely back in her pocket. She wasn't likely to get much more done today; she'd go back to the house and work some more on her report.

Rachel waded back to shore, mounted her bicycle, and set off again on the by now all too familiar access road. Rain began to fall steadily; gritting her teeth, she struggled to keep the bicycle on track.

She reached the house about half an hour later, steaming inside her raincoat. She remembered that a conference was booked in now, and took her bicycle round the side to park it out back. She draped her macintosh and hat over it, and left her muddy boots beside it. Slipping into the house, she padded in her stockinged feet round to the office.

A cold-drinks machine was groaning softly to itself in a corner by a little lounge—Grant had finally decided in favour of vending machines. Rachel realised suddenly that a cold drink would be wonderful. She'd stopped by the machine, and was digging money out of her pocket, when she heard voices.

'I'm sorry, Olivia, but there's nothing I can do.' Grant sounded unutterably weary. 'If you'd told me a few months ago it might have been different, but my capital's all tied up now and it'll be that way for a long while to come. It'll be five or, more likely, ten years before the park starts breaking even, never mind making a profit; I can't just take half a million out of it again at a moment's notice.'

'But Grant,' Olivia protested, 'half the reason my business is in trouble is that I've been down here when I should have been in London or Paris—I missed some crucial shows…'

There was a short pause. 'I'm sorry,' Grant said at last. 'I thought you were getting less interested in fashion and wanted to be more involved here. I'd never have asked you to sacrifice your business if I'd known. The problem is that at this stage to help you on the scale you need would jeopardise the science park, or at least mean postponing it for several years. I'd have to think about that very seriously— I couldn't possibly give you an answer now, when I'm leaving for New York in a couple of hours.'

This was getting worse and worse. Rachel wished desperately that she could somehow escape her hiding place unseen. She thought, briefly, of just walking out, and shuddered.

Olivia said nothing. After a moment Grant went on, 'I'd thought of putting you in charge here while I was away, but obviously this puts matters in a different perspective. You must want to be back in London now. Surely if you work at it single-mindedly without the distraction of my affairs, there's a good chance that you could pull it back from the brink?'

'I don't know,' said Olivia. 'That is—to tell the truth, Grant, I think my second-in-command can deal with things for now. I take it you'd pay a full-time salary if I ran things here—that would help me a bit—and I don't want you worrying about things while you're away. You're right, this is the important thing. I'll handle everything. Just leave everything to me.'

'I can't let you do that,' said Grant. 'You've done too much already.'

'No, I insist. Don't give it another thought.'

Grant gave a rather strained laugh. 'Well, I can't do that, but, if you're sure, I'll accept just temporarily—it would be hard to change at such short notice before I go. You're an angel to do it. As soon as I get back I'll make sure someone else is brought in to deal with everything here.'

At last they moved out of earshot. Rachel got a cold drink from the machine and went to her office to face the loathsome task of writing up.

She hadn't done much more than shade in a few squares of graph paper in an absent-minded doodle when the door opened and Grant came in.

'Where the hell have you been?' he demanded.

'I *was* standing up to my waist in water, letting the rain deal with the rest of me,' Rachel retorted. 'Then I came here to write up.'

'Hard at work, I see,' he said sarcastically, glancing at the sheet of paper. 'I thought I told you not to hire that idiot.'

'I *didn't*,' said Rachel.

'Well, I see you know who I meant,' he observed, with a sardonic grin. 'Everywhere I go I seem to fall over him. I thought you'd broken up. What happened, did you kiss and make up?'

Rachel fought down an urge to tell him to mind his own business or, even better, tell him that she was marrying Driscoll tomorrow. 'No,' she said patiently. 'We're still disengaged, and I did not put him on the payroll. It was Olivia's idea.'

Whatever he had been expecting it hadn't been this. 'Olivia!' he exclaimed incredulously. 'Why on earth would Olivia hire that blockhead?'

'She had some idea about making this an—an ecological haven for rare species,' said Rachel. 'She said she knew it was what you would want.'

Grant scowled. 'I'd rather we did the right thing by the habitats we've got,' he said. 'Why didn't you tell her?'

'Why should I?'' asked Rachel. 'She's your fiancée. The one who agrees with you on everything of importance, remember? If she says she knows what you want, who am I to disagree?'

Grant opened his mouth and then shut it, loyalty winning out over annoyance. 'Oh, well, I suppose he can't do any actual harm,' he said at last, grudgingly. 'I know Olivia meant well. Just don't get re-engaged while I'm away.'

'Away?' Rachel remembered just in time that this should come as a surprise.

'I'm going to the States for a month to talk to some potential investors.'

A month! Rachel thought in dismay. But it was already the first week of June—and the wedding was in August! The past few weeks hadn't been encouraging, but at least he'd been here. How could she possibly expect him to change his mind, though, if he didn't even see her?

'But what if something turns up in the EIA?' she asked.

'Is that likely?' he asked quickly. 'If there was a problem and the Press got onto it, it could kill investor interest pretty swiftly.'

'It's looking good so far,' said Rachel. 'But you never know. Still, if something does turn up I won't tell anyone but you.'

'You can tell Olivia. I'm leaving her in charge and she knows where to reach me.'

Rachel agreed reluctantly.

There was a long silence. Rachel braced herself for another barrage of criticism. Grant was staring down at her, the blue eyes unusually brilliant.

'Well, hope it all goes well,' he said at last. 'See you in a few weeks.' He hesitated. Then, to her astonishment, he kissed her on the cheek and walked abruptly out of the room.

The next week seemed to go smoothly enough. Rachel didn't know what Driscoll was doing for Olivia—the great thing was that she hardly ever saw him. Apparently he was doing something or other in the woodlands at the opposite end of the property. Rachel had been able to report on these using material already available; since no new research was needed she had only visited that part of the property once or twice.

On Friday evening, however, Rachel bicycled over to the house to find Olivia waiting for her. The blonde woman invited Rachel into Grant's office and sat down behind his desk, frowning.

'Rachel, I don't know how to put this, but I'm going to have to ask you to leave the survey.' She propped immaculately manicured fingers against each other. 'I'm asking

Driscoll to take over from next week, with staff if he needs it.'

'What?'

Olivia raised one beautifully plucked eyebrow. 'Apparently he's found a dozen endangered or at least rare species of insect in that woodland patch you decided we didn't need to survey, and a couple of rare plants.' She placed a sheet of paper with a list of Latin names in front of Rachel, then took it back before Rachel could look at it closely.

'He went over that waterway that you fell into the other day, and actually turned up a number of rare plants that must have been right under your nose.' Her eyes were cold. 'I suppose Grant shouldn't have insisted on your taking the contract; anyway, this standard of work isn't quite what he had in mind. I understand you've been wanting to get out ever since you started, so I hope you won't mind taking two weeks' pay in lieu of notice.'

Rachel opened her mouth and shut it. She had wanted to leave, of course, but she hated to leave a job half-done. She just couldn't understand it. She knew Driscoll wasn't nearly as painstaking as she was. Had he decided to show an excess of zeal just to impress, or because he was desperate for a job? It just defied belief, though, that she could have missed so much.

'As far as the waterway is concerned,' she said stiffly, 'it was raining very hard that day—so hard that I'd already decided I couldn't carry out any more observations on the areas I'd already selected for study. The fact that I may not have noticed something under poor conditions has nothing to do with my competence. Most of my work has been over strips of ground that I've conducted repeated surveys of, week in, week out. The whole point is to get enough data to produce meaningful statistics, which *allow* for the possibility that on some particular day you miscounted, or there were unusually high or low numbers to be counted.'

'And how do you explain the high numbers of rare species in areas you decided not to survey?' Olivia inquired.

'You don't do an ecological assessment by surveying every inch of the countryside from scratch,' Rachel explained patiently. 'You go through the information that's already available, pinpoint the areas that are likely to be affected and carry out new research if required.'

Olivia looked blank.

'There was no reason to think the waterway required any special attention,' Rachel insisted. 'Nothing in any of the existing data, and no striking features when we did the general survey. What you tell me is surprising, and odd, but I can assure you we've followed best practice.'

'Well, I'm afraid it's just not good enough,' said Olivia.

Rachel bit her lip. It went sorely against the grain to receive her dismissal from Olivia. What would she tell Grant? That Rachel hadn't been doing her job properly? That she'd walked out on it?

'Does Grant know about this?' she asked. 'As you say, he insisted on my taking the contract; I want to be quite sure he's agreed to release me from it.'

'Of course he knows about it,' said Olivia. 'I explained the situation to him, and he asked me to deal with it. He's extremely disappointed with the way you've carried out your assignment. Feel free to call him in New York if you want to—but remember that he's horribly busy just now. I'd have thought you could be responsible enough not to take up his time.'

'Of course,' said Rachel. 'But I think there must be some mistake.'

'I'm afraid the only mistake was ours in taking you on,' said Olivia severely. Rachel got the distinct impression that the other woman was enjoying herself. 'I'm sorry if that hurts your feelings, but there's rather a lot riding on this; it's extremely disturbing to see it put in jeopardy like this.'

'I can see it would be,' said Rachel quietly. 'Is there anything else?'

'Yes,' said Olivia, with a venomous look. 'You can take your bloody tarantula with you!'

In the white heat of her fury with Grant, Rachel found she was capable of superhuman feats that she could never have accomplished otherwise. She walked into her aunt's kitchen, glass case under her arm, and informed her aunt starkly that William would be staying with them in future. Aunt Harriet demurred, with violence and no little eloquence. Rachel repeated that William was staying, in her room, and stalked upstairs. If only all battles were so easily won!

CHAPTER TWELVE

RACHEL spent the next two weeks in what should have been the job of her dreams. She'd found an opening as a secretary at a local auction house, whose premises had not known live flora or fauna for at least five generations. She wore the beautiful clothes Grant had bought her. She typed correspondence at a respectable sixty words per minute, answered telephones and read *Vogue* in the many quiet moments.

Her employer, Mr Murcheson, was a perfect gentleman. He always let her leave punctually at five. He lent her umbrellas when it rained, and tut-tutted if she came in with wet feet. He did not sit on her desk; his interest in legs was confined to antique furniture; he would probably have fainted if she had suggested bringing in her pet tarantula. The problem was that she was bored.

Rachel wanted an employer who rushed in at five o'clock and insisted on talking about the metabolism of dinosaurs. She wanted someone who talked her ear off for three hours and then fed her on baked beans. She wanted someone who couldn't take his eyes off her legs, and threatened to undress her when she got wet. She wanted Grant.

No, she did not want Grant, she told herself every time she reached this unpleasant discovery. His wedding was only a month away. Besides, she was furious with him. How dared he leap to conclusions? How dared he accept what Driscoll said without verifying it? She hadn't thought he loved her, but she'd at least thought he liked her; how could he be so unreasonable?

Not that it made any difference to *her*. *She* didn't want to be standing in a swamp, or counting insects in a square metre of woodland. *She* hadn't *asked* to do his stupid project; *he* had forced *her* into it against her will.

But she was still furious. It was so obvious that something fishy was going on. Some of the species on the list were so improbable for the locale, and why had they all been turned up by Driscoll?

Sometimes she thought she was being paranoid—but didn't it look like a deliberate attempt to get her out of the way? Why? What was going on? Why hadn't Grant *seen* that something odd was going on and asked her to help him sort it out, instead of assuming *she* was to blame? And last, but by no means least, how *dared* he tell Olivia, of all people, to give her the sack? He could at least have had the decency to tell her himself!

Morosely, Rachel finished typing the morning's correspondence and took it in to Mr Murcheson. There was nothing else to do, and she'd finished *Vogue*, *Harper's* and *Marie Claire*, so she made a cup of tea and opened the office copy of the *Financial Times*. Her eyes drifted down the page; she raised the mug to her mouth, then put it down again while she read, frowning.

Her eyes had gravitated automatically to a piece on the British fashion industry. The article analysed the factors that had made a number of British companies successful, then pinpointed the weakness of others that had been going steadily downhill.

The days were gone, it said, when who you knew mattered more than what you did; it devoted a scathing paragraph to Olivia St Clair, who had tried to get by on snob value when others had been succeeding through hard work, imagination and sheer professionalism. According to the piece, St Clair's had been posting losses for the last five years, and had been on the brink of bankruptcy, though rumour had it that a fresh injection of capital had bailed out the firm.

No wonder Olivia had been so desperate for Grant to make a quick profit, Rachel thought. It didn't look as though it was involvement with Grant that had undermined the company, though. If anything, Rachel's baser self speculated, Olivia's sudden uncharacteristic interest in Amazonian tribes and in Grant looked like a bid to save herself. And there was poor Grant going on about shared idealism! The worst of it was that if this rumour was right it must mean that Grant had decided to help Olivia after all, even if it meant jeopardising his own project.

Rachel folded up the paper despondently and washed out her mug. Then she made another cup of tea. She rearranged the pile of saleroom catalogues on the waiting-room table, spreading them in an artistic little fan. There was still nothing to do.

In desperation she opened the *Financial Times* again—and this time she stared at the pale pink page in open-mouthed horror.

FINANCING STALLS FOR SCIENCE PARK was the headline; in a short column, the piece described investors as increasingly cautious about Arrowmead. Several rare plants and insects had been spotted on the premises by the environmentalist in charge, Dr Driscoll Parry. Now Dr Parry had identified a breeding pair of Savi's Warblers in an extensive reedbed on the property. There were thought to be fewer than twenty breeding pairs in the entire country; the sighting, if genuine, could significantly delay or limit planning permission. There was a serious possibility that the area might be considered suitable for a nature reserve in order to protect a rare breeding spot for the birds.

The article concluded on a more sinister note. Dr Parry, it said, had remarked that the male birds typically began singing in early May; he had expressed surprise that their

presence had not been noticed in the course of an in-depth
survey of the reedbed which his predecessor had been con-
ducting for the last two months. Financial analysts pre-
dicted that the implication of a possible cover-up would
further undermine investors' confidence in the scheme.

Rachel bit her lip. A *Savi's Warbler*? Spotted by *Driscoll*, who'd never been able to spot anything smaller than
a barn owl? Something was seriously wrong.

She remembered, suddenly, Olivia's promise to introduce Driscoll to Matheson. Suppose she'd done it? Driscoll
wanted a secure job—it wouldn't take much of an offer
from Matheson to persuade Driscoll to undermine the ecological impact assessment.

Well, however badly Grant had behaved, she didn't want
his project destroyed. If there was any possibility that he
was being sabotaged, she had to do what she could to expose it.

Rachel hesitated, then picked up the phone and dialled
the mansion. Could she speak to Mr Mallett? Mr Mallett
was in New York. No, there was no message.

Rachel couldn't quite face talking to Olivia over the
phone. Still, if Olivia was that desperate for the place to
turn a profit, surely she'd jump at the chance to prove the
sighting of rare species was a false alarm?

At last she forced herself to bicycle over to the conference centre after work. After a short argument with the
secretary, she was shown into the office.

'Yes, what is it?' Olivia didn't trouble to disguise her
boredom.

'I saw the piece in the *FT* about the rare species,' said
Rachel.

'Well?'

'The more I think about this, the fishier it looks,' Rachel
persevered. 'Could someone be trying to destroy Grant? I
think those rare species may have been planted...'

No need to say she thought Driscoll was responsible. It

was *possible* someone else had done it. It was *possible* he'd just seen a small bird and misidentified it. It was even possible he'd seen a small bird and identified it correctly, but if so it would be for the first time in his life.

'You mean the plants, I take it,' Olivia said curtly. 'Are you implying that Driscoll deliberately manufactured false sightings of the birds as well?'

So much for protecting Driscoll. 'No, but misidentifications aren't as uncommon as you'd think,' said Rachel uncomfortably. 'Anyway, you can't prove that one way or the other, whereas you *can* prove it if the plants aren't native. All you have to do is get soil samples from close to the roots of the plants and from the surrounding ground, and compare them—my bet is they'll be different.'

Olivia tapped her pencil on the desk. 'That's wonderful news if it's true,' she said. 'But obviously we don't want to get Grant's hopes up. I'd rather we didn't tell him until we were sure.'

'Of course,' said Rachel. 'But mightn't we want to spread a counter-rumour? I mean, isn't it worth keeping the share prices up if we can?'

'If we act rashly we may make things worse,' Olivia said obscurely.

'Well, at least let me have a look,' said Rachel. 'Driscoll must have drawn up a map showing where he saw these things. Let me get some soil samples and have a look at the context to see if anything looks suspicious.'

Olivia inspected her nails. 'I think we ought to get in an independent assessor, to be perfectly honest,' she said, in her bored, drawling voice. 'After all, it's not as if you don't have a vested interest in this. These discoveries have put a question mark over your professional competence, and, to be perfectly frank, what's to stop you from collecting fake samples, or even destroying the plants, just to protect yourself? I'm not saying you *would* do it, but the possibility's there, and we can't be too careful.'

'That's a ridiculous suggestion!' Rachel said hotly.

Olivia shrugged. 'You must try to see my position,' she said smoothly. 'I'm afraid I'm going to have to ask you not to come on the grounds without prior permission. Of course I'll arrange for someone else to come in. Meanwhile, if there is nothing further you want to discuss...'

Rachel shook her head in frustration. If she could only believe that Olivia would do something, it wouldn't really matter who made the investigation...but would she?

Well, it wouldn't hurt if it was done twice, she decided.

'No, that's all,' she said, with a bright, false smile, and left the room before she could say anything impolite.

Rachel's first move was to go instantly to the small room which had once been her office. Her bet was that Driscoll would have gone home for the day—Driscoll did not like working long hours. So with any luck she could unearth a copy of the list and the map herself...

Finding them was easy. They could hardly be hidden when they were supposed to be part of perfectly genuine research; Driscoll had simply started a new tab in the lever arch file and inserted the papers behind it.

Now came the hard part. Rachel extracted the papers from the file and tiptoed across the corridor to the photo-copier. The map had to be darkened and reduced, and the list was double-sided; at each groan of the machine she was sure she'd be discovered.

No one came, however, and five minutes later she was outside, heart pounding, the precious pages stuffed into a pocket.

If there was one thing Rachel hated more than anything else in the world, it was getting up early in the morning, but for Grant she would even do that. She spent the evening going through her research books reading up on the species on Driscoll's list, making copious notes on the features one would expect to find in their surroundings; then, with a grimace, she set her alarm for five a.m.

The morning was grey and cold, with a mist that would probably lift later in the day. Rachel stuffed her notes and a camera into a backpack, then set off on her trusty bicycle.

It took twenty minutes to cover the five miles to the back entrance to the property, and forty minutes of furious pedalling over the rutted access road to go the next two miles to the turn-off to the woods. The road branched off by the waterway and became little more than a pair of tracks climbing through the trees. Noise was deadened by the thick carpet of leaves; there was something a little spooky about the silent road disappearing ahead in the mist between ranks of fog-shrouded trees.

Atmosphere was irrelevant, Rachel told herself sternly. The important thing was the job at hand. She dismounted and leant her bicycle against a tree, and with a show of scientific matter-of-factness took out Driscoll's map and opened it up to get her bearings.

As she did so a sharp chill ran down her back—in her mind's eye Rachel saw, with horrible vividness, the first, unreduced copy of the map which she'd made and put to one side and forgotten to take with her. What if it was found? What if someone suspected she was here? Suddenly the forest seemed full of mysterious rustling noises, as if someone was lurking just out of sight. A branch scraped across a tree trunk; Rachel whirled around, heart beating violently, then sighed with relief when she saw the branch swaying in the wind.

At last she forced herself to shake off these nerves. Working her way down the list, with the map as a guide, she tried to find what Driscoll had seen. A couple of the items had withered to limp little clumps of vegetation; Rachel took pictures, and scooped soil samples into plastic envelopes. There were no Savi's Warblers, naturally—the bird was a great skulker, and skulked exclusively in reedbeds even when somebody hadn't just pretended to see it. None of the rare insects were to be seen either, but she took pictures of the places where they were supposed to have appeared.

At last there was only one plant left on the list. Rachel strode through the undergrowth and clambered over fallen trees, following Driscoll's map. Once or twice she stopped, startled by a crackling sound behind her—but when she listened and looked back she heard only the wind in the leaves overhead.

She started again—and now she felt an odd prickling at the back of her neck, as though she were being followed. She looked around, but there was no one to be seen; that was what came of an over-active imagination, she told herself.

She stepped at last out into the clearing marked on the map. Resolutely she knelt down beside the wilted leaves and drooping purple blossom which had once been a Lady Orchid. There was a violent blow on the back of her head—and everything went black.

CHAPTER THIRTEEN

RACHEL woke in a room she had never seen before. She was lying, feet tied at the ankles, wrists tied behind her back, on a dusty mattress on a rusting bed; above her head a sharply gabled roof suggested that she was in an attic. There was a throbbing pain in her head, and her arms protested against her uncomfortable position; she wished she hadn't come to. She supposed she should consider herself lucky she hadn't been gagged. This wasn't entirely comforting, however, since this must mean her captors thought there was no danger of anyone hearing her if she did cry out.

Sunlight streamed through a window onto the far wall. She had no idea how long she'd been unconscious, and as she didn't know which direction the room faced she was unable to guess the time. She lay on her side, trying to work out what had happened and why, but her brain was too weary. She closed her eyes and fell asleep again.

She woke again in semi-darkness. Her arms felt as though someone had stabbed them with red-hot wires; her neck and shoulders were cramped and stiff. There was still no sign of her captors. There was nothing to do but wait, and hope they had not abandoned her altogether. She lay for an indefinite period staring into the gathering darkness, wondering whether she would ever see Grant again, until at last she slept…

The next time she woke suddenly, as something heavy

dropped onto the bed beside her. The room was still dark, too dark to see.

The door closed, the lock turned. She was left on the bed with—something. Something human, anyway, for it was breathing heavily. Rachel had not thought it possible to be more uncomfortable, but now, jammed against the wall by this temporarily lifeless body, she found it impossible to sleep.

Slowly the dark thinned, then lightened to a grainy black, then to grey. Gradually she was able to see the features of her fellow captive. It was Grant.

There was a dark smear on one side of his head that looked like blood; the dark blond hair was matted with it. A thin film of sweat glistened on his skin; she didn't know whether that was a good or bad sign. He was unshaven, the dark bristles thick on his jaw—not that that was a sign of anything but an unusually long separation from his razor, but it was so at odds with his usual casually debonair appearance that it made her uneasy too.

Still, there was nothing she could do for him. Like her, he seemed to be tied hand and foot. He, too, would probably have a splitting headache when he woke; he might as well sleep as long as he could.

Even as she thought it, his eyes opened and met hers. Their expression was perplexed.

'Rachel?'

'Are you all right?' she asked softly.

'Rachel,' he said again. His head was beside hers on the mattress; he lifted it, seeming surprised that he couldn't move his arms. His eyes stared into hers; suddenly his head bent towards hers and he kissed her hungrily.

Other things being equal, Rachel would have thought this as good a way of passing the time as any, and better than most. After all, it wasn't as though they were going anywhere. But what on earth was going on? Grant had been as good as, or rather worse than, his word in maintaining an icy formality ever since the party.

Still, looking on the bright side, her headache had magically disappeared.

His chin rasped against hers, but his mouth was soft and warm. How long it had been since she'd tasted it! Perhaps he thought they were going to be killed. If they couldn't literally die in each other's arms, they could have the next best thing. Rachel responded enthusiastically, hampered by the awkwardness of holding her neck up.

She realised, suddenly, that something was not quite right. He kept rolling jerkily towards her, flailing his bound body on the bed as if in a terrible effort to get closer to her. His mouth was almost desperate, pushing against hers until her head was backed right up against the wall. Then a violent movement of his body shook his head sharply back. His eyes closed briefly, then opened wide.

'Rachel!' he said incredulously. And then, as realisation hit him, 'Oh, my God!'

The room was a little lighter now. Rachel could see the dull tide of crimson staining his cheeks.

'Rachel, I'm sorry. I don't know what to say. What the hell is going on?'

'I don't know,' said Rachel, trying to ignore the fact that her pulse seemed to be up to twice its normal speed. 'I went to collect some soil samples, and—I think I must have been hit over the head. One minute I was putting some soil in an envelope, the next minute I woke up here. What are you doing here? I thought you were in New York.'

'I was. Then I read in the paper that a lot of protected species were turning up here, so planning permission was likely to be refused for further development. Share prices were going through the floor. I thought I'd better get back and see what was going on.'

Now that he was really awake his eyes were suddenly chilling. 'Olivia told me you'd quit—'

'She *what*?'

'Does that mean you didn't?' His eyes softened slightly.

'She told me to go because they'd found all this new stuff which she said I'd overlooked. She told me you knew all about it!' Rachel said furiously. 'And then when I said I thought something suspicious was going on, and we should investigate, she said I might be trying to protect my reputation and she didn't trust me to do it myself.'

There was a glimmer of a smile in the dark blue eyes, though she had the impression that his head was hurting. 'So naturally you went quietly home to seek solace in *Vogue*...'

Rachel flushed. 'I just had to be sure, Grant. I thought there was no time to lose. I wasn't sure how long it would take Olivia to find someone else.'

He was frowning. 'So—let me get this straight—you're saying all these species might have been deliberately planted?'

'There's just something wrong about it, Grant,' she said. 'It's all so—so ostentatious.'

'What do you mean?'

'Well, all these things turning up that a non-ecologist could understand,' she explained. 'I mean, a survey might turn up all kinds of things that I'd find worrying. Your science park might have an impact on some extremely common water plant, for instance, that was the main food of an insect that was the main food of a bird that wasn't rare but was found in only a few places.'

She frowned. 'It seems to me that's already too complicated for the average investor to be instantly worried, and that's a *simplified* example of what I'd be looking for. Whereas a rare bird, or a rare plant, is so *obvious*. It's so easy to leak to the Press.'

'By Jove, Holmes!'

'I should have seen it before,' she admitted. 'But I *could* have overlooked something. It was only when the paper said that *Driscoll* had spotted a Savi's Warbler that I smelled a rat.'

'Not one of our leading birdwatchers, then?'

'No,' she said shortly. After a moment she added, reluctantly, 'I think Olivia introduced him to Mr Matheson, and I wondered... That is, there probably isn't much he wouldn't do to get a job.'

Grant tactfully refrained from making another of his pungent comments on Driscoll.

'I got my secretary to fax the list of plants and the map to me in New York,' he commented, abruptly changing the subject. 'I went straight to your uncle's house the minute I got back—I wanted you to tell me what the hell was going on. Then he told me you weren't there, but he thought you'd gone to the woods, so I just went after you. Then I found your bike leaning against a tree trunk.

'I started looking around. There seemed to have been something dragged along at one place. I started following the trail—there was a lot of broken undergrowth—and someone attacked me. I think I gave a pretty good account of myself, but someone hit me over the head, end of story. Next thing I knew I was here...' His face reddened again.

'I'm sorry about just now,' he said awkwardly—when had she ever seen Grant awkward? 'I—I've been having these dreams where I see you and try to get to you but I can't, or I get there too late. You know how in dreams you just do what you want...it was like one of those. My head must have been a bit unhinged after the blow—'

'Thank you,' said Rachel.

'You know what I mean. Anyway, how was I to know it wasn't a dream? The way you kissed me back was more like a fantasy than a lot of fantasies I've had.'

'I'm sorry,' said Rachel, not very repentantly. 'Do I look like a mind-reader? I thought it was odd, but you seemed to want to—who was I to object? It seemed a good way to pass the time. After all, there's not much else to do. And anyway, if this is the end of the road, we might as well enjoy the time we've got left. Our captors don't seem very interested in us. I haven't eaten in twenty-four hours—I thought you thought we might as well die happy.'

Grant grinned suddenly, then winced. It occurred to Rachel that he actually looked a lot more cheerful now, having been knocked over the head, wounded, tied hand and foot and probably left for dead, than he had comfortably playing chief executive behind a big desk. That was probably why he'd looked so oppressed, she decided. A man who was used to being shot at on a regular basis did not thrive on a milk-and-water diet of angry faxes.

Just look at him! His eyes were sparkling. A week or so of starvation, with maybe the odd beating thrown in, and he'd probably be spouting limericks and telling knock-knock jokes. If only, if only they had put him in a separate bedroom. Well, maybe not that exactly, she amended, remembering the kiss. But did he have to look so happy?

'Well, if we have to die I can't think of a better way to go,' he said. 'But I don't think it's that desperate. All we've got to do is untie ourselves and get out of here, and there won't be much they can do.'

'"All",' said Rachel.

'We clear out, find some breakfast, and see what the hell is going on. Wonder if they took your soil samples? We may have to go back for more.'

'"We",' said Rachel.

'I wouldn't want you to miss out on the fun,' said Grant. 'After all, it was your idea.'

'It's not my idea of fun to get hit over the head and be tied hand and foot,' said Rachel. 'It's all right for you—at least you haven't been here since yesterday morning.'

He smiled. 'Poor darling. All right, all the more reason to get on with step one.'

'And how do you suggest we do that?' said Rachel.

'Don't tell me, your Apache blood brother taught you this trick for escaping from bonds.'

'No—'

'Your grandfather was Houdini.'

'Unfortunately not—'

'You're the Incredible Shrinking Man.'

'Will you be quiet? It's perfectly simple. Turn around and face the wall, and I'll untie your wrists with my teeth. Then you can untie mine, and we'll do our own feet.'

'Can you really do that?' asked Rachel.

'Try me.' He smiled. 'Turn over now, and just leave the rest to me.'

Rachel rolled over, painfully, onto her other side. The bed shook wildly as Grant tried to manoeuvre himself into position, then fell to the floor.

After an interval of rather choice language, the bed shook again as he leant forward. Rachel could feel the rope being tugged at her wrists; she bit her lip to keep from crying out. A very, very long time went by.

Rachel lost track of time. It must have been a good two hours later, she estimated, when he at last said, 'OK, that should do it.'

She pulled one arm up, slowly, with excruciating pain— yes, she was free. She rolled onto her back, allowing her arms simply to lie at her sides, and looked at Grant.

'Grant!' she cried in horror. 'Are you all right?'

His face was pale, the blue eyes stark. His mouth was scraped and raw where he had struggled with the rope.

'Never better,' he managed.

Rachel forced herself to ignore the pain in her arms. She sat up and swung her feet to the floor. Grant needed to lie down as soon as possible. She could not waste time recovering.

'Turn around and I'll do you,' she said. He turned away. Gritting her teeth, Rachel moved her hands, in which circulation was unpleasantly returning, to the knots behind his back. They were tight, and intricately tied; with still numb fingers they were not easy to untie, and it took her a good twenty minutes to set him free.

They untied their ankles and stamped their feet softly on the floor to get the blood flowing.

'What happens now?' asked Rachel. Her arms were throbbing painfully, but she realised, with surprise, that she felt more at ease than she had for weeks. At least Grant was beside her. At least he wasn't giving her his granite-jawed routine.

'Well—if they come back soon, we lie back to back, hands behind us, and hope they don't look too carefully. Otherwise, there are three options. One, wait till we're in working order and overpower them. Two, break down the door. Three, escape by the window. I won't know which it has to be till I've had a look at two and three.'

Rachel thought about his drawn white face, the tight mouth.

'Won't that be rather difficult?' she said. 'I don't mean to be a wet blanket, but it seems to me it would be hard enough to do any of those things in peak condition. I don't know about you, but I feel that being hit on the head, tied up for hours and starved hasn't left me with the kind of energy I'd want to overpower someone, break down a door or escape through the window of an attic.'

'Shame on you, Spidergirl,' he said lightly. 'I'm relying on you to fell at least ten opponents at a blow, or *at least* go down the sheer side of a building without a rope. This defeatism ill becomes a superhero.'

'You're the superhero,' said Rachel. 'I never thought you'd be able to untie me. Is your mouth all right?'

'It'll do.'

'It looks terrible,' said Rachel candidly. 'Would you like me to kiss it better?'

There was a short silence. At last he said, 'You know I would, Spidergirl. There's not much point in pretending I wouldn't, now, is there? But you know life's not as simple as that.' He stood up abruptly, gripping the bedstead, then made his way step by painful step to the window. 'We've got to get out of here,' he said. 'These people have attacked anyone who's tried to get a look at that blasted wood. Meanwhile Olivia's out there with "Get in independent environmental assessor" on her list of things to do—there's absolutely no guarantee that they won't go for her first.'

Rachel bit her lip. She had begun to entertain a terrible suspicion. There had been no sign of Driscoll at Arrowmead when she'd copied the map; Olivia was the only person who knew she thought something was wrong. It was *possible* that Driscoll had come back—but there was a much simpler explanation of what had happened. She couldn't point the finger at her rival, though, so she made no comment, simply walking over to join Grant at the window.

'Where are we?' They were looking out over treetops with a long alley down the middle.

Rachel shook her head. 'I don't know. But I do know plan three is out of the question. We're on the fourth floor.'

'Oh, I don't know,' said Grant. 'If we've got enough rope I might be able to get up onto the roof.' He actually sounded as though he was looking forward to giving it a try, Rachel thought in disgust. 'You know,' he added, 'break into another window, get back into the house that way.' He held his hands up, measuring the window, and scowled—there was no way those broad shoulders could get through. 'Well, maybe I couldn't,' he said regretfully. '*You* could probably get through,' he offered generously.

'No,' said Rachel. 'Thanks, but no thanks.'

'Well, let's have a look at the door, then.'

The door appeared to be made of solid oak, and to have hinges on the outside.

Grant bent to listen at the keyhole, then straightened with

another grimace. He pushed against it experimentally with a shoulder and shook his head.

'Not a hope,' he said. 'Well, we're not going anywhere fast, and if anyone comes after us now we're in no shape to give them any trouble. Come over to the bed and lie on your stomach.'

'What?'

'You won't be up to much with those arms—how are your shoulders?'

'In agony,' said Rachel.

'Ever the stoic,' he said, grinning. 'Well, I'll see what I can do. Come on.'

Rachel obediently lay down on the bed again, and he began very gently kneading her shoulders.

She groaned. 'Don't stop,' she said. 'You're killing me, but it feels marvellous.'

'Good.' His hands were strong, the thumbs circling with slow, ever increasing pressure on the sore muscles. Slowly she felt the knots in her neck and back and shoulders dissolve. After a while she realised that she could quite happily have allowed this to go on for hours—but Grant should not be doing this indefinitely.

'That's much better,' she said regretfully at last. 'But this can't be good for you.' She groaned again appreciatively. 'If anyone has to fell an opponent it'll probably be you. You'd better let me work on you for a while.'

There was another silence. She got the impression that he wasn't entirely happy with the suggestion, but he could not argue with its good sense. 'All right,' he said. 'You're right, I'm probably not good for much yet.'

'Oh, I wouldn't say that,' Rachel said. She turned over and sat up. 'You'll have to take off your shirt,' she told him.

'*What?*'

'*I* only got hit over the head; *you* got beaten up,' she

said reasonably. 'If you keep your shirt on I might hit a bruise. I don't want to hurt you.'

Grant growled something under his breath.

'Do you want me to do it for you?' she asked.

'No, that's all right,' he said hastily. He unbuttoned his shirt, glaring at Rachel, tossed it to the floor with another glare at the ministering angel, and lay down again.

'You don't mind if I sit on your back, do you?' asked Rachel. 'If I have to lean over at an odd angle I think I may strain my muscles again.'

Grant sighed. 'Why did it always seem like a *bad* dream when you were inaccessible?' he asked. 'I should have quit when I was ahead. Maybe we should just forget about it.'

'But Grant,' objected Rachel, 'we *can't* forget about it. I'm relying on you to protect me.'

'Yes,' said Grant. 'So I see. Now if only I had someone to protect me from you I'd feel a lot better. All right, do your damnedest.'

Rachel promptly straddled his back, kneeling on the narrow bed, and lowered herself to sit at the base of his spine. She began massaging the tight muscles of his neck and shoulders, working at them with her knuckles.

He drew in his breath sharply, then let it out again. Rachel supposed she should be nervous—after all, at any moment violent, ruthless kidnappers might burst into the room, and you could bet they would not take well to the spectacle of their captives giving each other massages. Still, she reasoned, neither she nor Grant could do anything anyway if they couldn't move.

She continued to knead away at the hard, muscular back, gradually working her way down the spine and back up again. There were a couple of pretty spectacular bruises, which she did her best to avoid; once he flinched as she inadvertently touched a tender spot, but for the most part he lay rigid and unmoving on the bed.

'Am I hurting you?' she asked at last, wondering whether he was steeling himself not to show pain.

'No,' said Grant through gritted teeth. 'Killing with kindness, maybe.'

Rachel ignored this. He felt *wonderful*—the skin silky, smooth over the lean muscle, the narrow waist rising to broad, powerful shoulders.

At last, reluctantly, she stopped. Too bad she didn't have an excuse to take off some more of his clothes, she thought regretfully. 'They didn't injure you on the leg, did they?' she asked hopefully, getting to her feet.

'No,' said Grant. 'And if they had I wouldn't tell you. None of this petticoats-into-bandages nonsense from you, Dr Hawkins.'

'I don't have a petticoat,' said Rachel.

'And I don't have a leg wound, thank God for small mercies.' He slipped into his shirt again.

'Maybe we'll have to overpower them after all,' Rachel said unenthusiastically. 'If they ever show up.' She couldn't decide which was worse—engaging in unarmed combat with a modern-day Neanderthal, or just being left to starve here. She'd had some chocolate in her backpack, but there was no sign of it; not only were her notes and camera in the hands of the enemy, they also had her Cadbury's Fruit and Nut. These people were obviously fiendishly clever: she thought she could have put up some kind of a fight if she'd just had breakfast. Or at least if she'd had breakfast, lunch, tea, dinner and breakfast...

'Well, it's what I'd like best,' Grant said grimly. 'I wouldn't mind getting a bit of my own back, not to mention getting even with the bastard who hit you.'

Well, at least someone would enjoy it, Rachel thought morosely. 'What do you want me to do if they do come?' she asked.

'Stay out of the way.'

It was what she'd wanted to hear, but as soon as he said

it she was furious. 'There might be lots of them!' she protested.

'I don't want to have to be worrying about you on top of—'

He was interrupted by the sound of footsteps in the corridor outside the room.

Grant was on his feet in an instant, gesturing to Rachel to stand behind him. She stepped back. The door opened a fraction—and Grant hurled himself against it, crushing the unseen visitor between door and wall.

Rachel approached the doorway in time to see the jailer slide out from behind the door, receive a single, powerful blow on the jaw from Grant, and collapse to the floor.

She stared, bemused, at the unconscious figure. One minute they'd been captives for who knew how long, now the door was open, their captor was in a deep faint and it was all over.

'Right, let's get him inside,' said Grant, putting his hands under the victim's armpits. Rachel took his feet. They deposited the body on the bed and used the ropes to secure him. Grant stripped off the mask the man was wearing and stared at his face.

'Do you recognise him?' asked Rachel.

'Well, he's one of the thugs who attacked me yesterday. Never seen him before that in my life.'

CHAPTER FOURTEEN

'I've always wanted to have the chance to say, We have ways of making you talk,' said Grant, looking down at their captive. 'But we don't have any time to waste.' He shook his head regretfully. 'He didn't bring any food with him, so he must have been on some other errand. They'll be expecting him back.'

'So when he doesn't show, sooner or later they'll send someone to see what's happened,' said Rachel.

'Exactly.'

'And we don't want to be here when reinforcements arrive,' she added emphatically.

'Well, I don't want you to be here,' he amended. 'Anyway, chances are, he doesn't know anything very useful. He's just a strongman. We need to go to headquarters.'

'We need to go to the police,' said Rachel.

'Oh—yes, of course,' said Grant. 'The police. Obviously. I just want to find out what's going on first.'

'I was thinking we could leave that to the police,' said Rachel, not very hopefully. She didn't like the way Grant's eyes were sparkling. He was undoubtedly having the time of his life. He did not look like a man about to let the police have all the fun.

Grant gave her a rather rueful smile. 'You think I just don't want to let someone else in on the fun, don't you?' he asked, with his old uncanny trick of reading her mind.

'Well...' Rachel searched for a tactful reply.

'In other words, yes.' He grinned. 'Well, I won't deny

it's more fun than boardroom politics. There's a serious reason behind it, though.' He raised an eyebrow. 'I'm not just worried about a bump on the head, you know. I've got a business to think about. I've got to have as much information as I can if I'm to fight this out.'

'Which the police—'

'Won't necessarily be able to release to me.' He shrugged. 'I can't afford to wait for it all to come out in the wash. By that time someone may have taken over my business.'

Rachel wasn't fooled for a moment by his responsible tone of voice. She knew he was having a marvellous time. The thing she couldn't work out was how much *he'd* worked out. Surely it was obvious who had had the best opportunity to do all this?

Of course, it might be that Grant realised Olivia was likely to be involved, she reflected. That might be another reason why he was reluctant to go to the police. He might want to spare her if he could. Meanwhile, loyalty might prevent him from mentioning what could only be a suspicion to Rachel. If he really thought Olivia was involved, though, how could he possibly sound so cheerful?

Whatever the truth of the matter, she realised, she couldn't possibly press him on it. 'So what do we do?' she asked. 'Conceal ourselves in a secret passageway that just happens to be outside the room where the conspirators are conspiring? Loiter until we overhear the secret password and then smuggle ourselves into the meeting in disguise?'

'I don't know yet. I'll wait for inspiration.'

'Another of your great hunches.'

'Absolutely.' He grinned again. 'Meanwhile I want you to go home. I don't want to endanger you any further, and if there's fighting I may not be able to protect you.'

Rachel argued hotly against this, but Grant, usually so easygoing, was adamant. 'All right, then,' she said at last.

'If I can't go with you I'll call the police the minute I get home.'

Grant scowled. 'But you don't even like adventures!' he protested. 'You're starving. You know you'd rather be having a hot bath.'

'I'm going with you,' said Rachel. 'I'd rather be with you than sitting in a hot bath wondering what's happened to you. Anyway, if you have me to think of maybe you won't be quite so foolhardy.'

'That's what I'm afraid of,' he complained.

'Good. Then that's settled,' said Rachel. She knew she was every kind of fool to insist on going along when Grant had given her an easy way out. She didn't like being hit on the head. She didn't like being tied up. For all she knew, people might shoot at them, and she didn't think she'd like that either. What was more, she didn't want the chance to find out. Anything was better, though, than sitting at home imagining the worst. Grant locked the door of the room behind them, and they made their way quietly along an attic corridor.

He listened intently for a moment at the head of a flight of stairs, then crept noiselessly down. Rachel followed, her heart in her mouth.

To her annoyance Grant didn't even look nervous. His eyes were practically throwing off blue sparks, his lean, tough body had the kind of unthinking alertness that Rachel associated with predatory animals. Well, at least one of them was enjoying himself, she thought sourly.

There was no sound on this floor. Grant padded silently down the next flight of stairs, his reluctant sidekick gloomily bringing up the rear.

Wherever they were, it was huge and old, and its owner was fantastically rich. They were looking down a corridor covered with what looked like priceless carpets, and lined with suits of armour and portraits of eighteenth-century horses and cases of Chinese vases and other treasures.

Grant hesitated, then set off to explore—and almost immediately discovered that there were a few expensive humans about as well.

They hadn't passed more than three or four doors when they had to hide behind a suit of armour while a maid in a black uniform crossed the corridor with an armful of towels. They were about to go on when what looked like a genuine butler, with an actual decanter on an actual silver salver, came up the stairs and proceeded at a stately pace towards them. Luckily he turned aside to enter a room a few doors down, and, on emerging, returned the way he had come.

Grant jerked his head at the door. 'Maybe something going on in there we should know about,' he whispered. 'Come on.' He moved silently across the corridor to the door next to the one the butler had used, and after listening a moment opened it carefully and slipped inside.

Rachel followed, relieved to be out of that long, dangerous corridor. She had no time to take in the magnificence of their new surroundings. Grant was already at the window. She could see his reasoning: they could hear the murmur of voices next door, but no words—if the window was open next door they might catch more.

Grant eased open the window and listened carefully. A few phrases could be heard—someone said angrily, 'Look, I've done my part and I want to know when I'll be paid!'

There was a murmur they couldn't hear, and then someone else said in exasperation, 'What in God's name possessed you to come here? I can't be seen to be involved!'

But then the voices dropped, as if both had remembered the need for discretion. Grant scowled.

'Now what do we do?' asked Rachel. 'Listen at the keyhole?'

Grant shook his head. 'Too risky.'

Oh, good, Rachel thought with relief. Now they'd get out of here and call the police. She'd actually started walking back to the door when she realised that Grant wasn't with her. Not only was he not with her but he was halfway out of the window; she was just in time to see his remaining leg swing over the windowsill and disappear.

She went to the window and found that Grant was now inching his way along a narrow ledge which ran the length of the building. Of course, that would be his idea of playing safe, she thought indignantly.

At first she simply watched, at once fascinated and horrified. The ledge couldn't have been more than a few inches wide, and the smooth brickwork of the house gave nothing to grip. Rachel was deliberately not looking down, but she knew perfectly well that there was a hard marble pavement below. Grant, however, was moving as easily as if there were a foot-wide surface beneath his feet and a drop of a few inches behind him.

He was already several feet away, and there was nothing Rachel could do to help. Gritting her teeth, she clenched her fists in her pockets. One gripped a waterproof pen, the other... The other, she realised, had closed on her tiny tape recorder.

Rachel bit her lip in frustration. Grant was too far away for her to hand him the recorder, and she obviously couldn't call out to him, and... Rachel looked bitterly down at the ground, which seemed to be an awfully long way away. There was only one thing to do. She would have to go after him.

Rachel swung a leg over the window-sill and lowered herself gingerly down. Gripping the sill, she brought over her other leg. Her feet were about four sizes smaller than Grant's, she reminded herself. On the other hand, one of the two people could fill a generously shaped brassière, and it happened to be the one who didn't like heights. Never mind, she told herself bracingly. Years from now you'll look back on this and laugh.

Making sure the tape recorder was in the pocket nearest

Grant, Rachel began inching her way along the ledge. He was right about one thing, anyway—you could hear the voices loud and clear. She'd already set the tape recorder going; she just hoped it was picking this up.

'Where the hell is Mallett? We can't do anything without him.' It was a man's voice—one that sounded vaguely familiar.

'I keep telling you I don't know!' The frustrated, petulant voice was unmistakably Olivia's. 'I talked to him on the phone a few nights ago and he seemed fine. Then when I called his hotel after the story broke they didn't know where he'd gone.'

'Well, keep trying, will you? The takeover can't go through unless he releases some shares; the board is relying on you to do your part.'

'Oh, he'll listen to me,' Olivia said confidently. 'He always does what I say sooner or later.'

'He wasn't very co-operative about Glomac's original approach,' the interlocutor's voice said sceptically, and Rachel suddenly recognised it as Matheson's.

'He has an idealistic streak, but obviously when the company's value has plummeted he'll see he has no choice.' Olivia's tone was slightly contemptuous; Rachel couldn't imagine what it must be like for Grant to hear this. She just wished he didn't have to hear it standing over a forty-foot drop.

'Assuming we can keep the story running long enough. I'm worried about all these people who keep nosing around. All it takes is one journalist to get a close look at these alleged rare species on site...' Matheson fretted. 'Where the hell is Griffiths, anyway?' he demanded irritably. 'We sent him to look in on them half an hour ago. We know about the girl, but who's this man they've brought in?'

'How should I know?' snapped Olivia.

'The whole thing has been a shambles from first to last,' Matheson complained. 'This should never have happened—if Parry had stuck to insects instead of planting things that died on the spot, we'd have nothing to worry about.'

'But Olivia *told* me to go ahead with the plants.'' Rachel knew that voice anyway—it was Driscoll at his most aggrieved.

'Yes,' Olivia agreed bitterly. 'Because you told me you could make it look convincing. Obviously if you'd been able to get the things to grow we'd have preferred solid evidence to asking people to take your word for what you'd seen.'

That was exactly what they needed, Rachel thought. If only she could be sure the tape recorder was getting it all! Clinging precariously to the wall with her left hand, she moved her right hand to her pocket and brought out the tiny recorder. She was afraid of startling Grant, but she slowly stretched out her hand in the direction of the window.

She must have made some slight noise. Grant's head whipped round. His eyes met Rachel's for one blistering moment before shifting to the tape recorder she held towards him.

That single furious glance was enough. Rachel's eyes flinched away from his—and she made the mistake of accidentally looking down.

Her head swam at the sight of the ground, far below. If only Grant would take the tape recorder so she could cling to the wall! She teetered wildly on the ledge, and for one terrible moment thought she was actually going to fall backwards—but suddenly her arm was anchored against the wall. Grant's hand gripped her wrist, holding her steady, and the tape recorder slipped from her hand to smash on the marble forty feet down.

'What was that?' Olivia asked sharply. 'I heard something.'

'The window's loose in the next room,' said Matheson.

'The wind must have shaken it. You're letting your nerves get to you.'

'I heard something, I tell you,' Olivia insisted.

'This is a waste of time.' Matheson was impatient. 'I don't know why you came over here. You'd better get back to Arrowmead; if Mallett tries to get in touch I want you there.'

'Yes, but—'

'I'll be in touch with you in due course, Dr Parry,' Matheson added, his voice smooth. 'In the meantime, I can't emphasise enough that discretion is everything in a matter like this; if you jeopardise my position again by coming here I shall consider myself released of all obligations towards you and take steps accordingly. Do I make myself clear?'

Driscoll mumbled something.

'I'll see you both out,' Matheson added pleasantly, 'and then have a word with Griffiths. I'm extremely annoyed that you had him bring these people here, Parry. I thought Miss St Clair might need his services; that doesn't mean I want him to turn up on my doorstep with everything he catches.'

Chairs scraped on the floor, footsteps crossed the room. A door opened, and shut.

Rachel held Grant's eyes in desperation. She knew she couldn't go back the way she'd come. But soon people would be coming out of the house; they'd only have to look up to see a couple of human flies plastered to its side, and if they saw the dropped tape recorder they'd be bound to look up.

'Don't worry,' Grant mouthed to her silently. 'Come this way.'

Still gripping her wrist, he inched along the ledge to the window of the vacated room. He glanced inside to make sure the coast was clear, then held onto the window-frame while Rachel steadily edged towards him.

When she had both hands on the window-sill he swung inside, then grasped both her wrists and pulled her in. His blue eyes were shooting sparks again, though probably not because he was having a wonderful time. He looked furious.

'Ever done any climbing before?' he asked.

'No,' Rachel admitted. 'But I thought we should get a recording of what they were saying. I'm sorry I dropped the tape recorder; why didn't you grab it?'

'Why do you think?' he retorted.

'There was absolutely no need to hold onto me,' Rachel informed him. 'I'd have been fine if I'd had my hand free.'

Grant scowled at her, his blue eyes crackling with annoyance. For a moment she thought he'd argue the point; then he remembered where they were.

'Let's get out of here,' he said tersely.

They checked that the coast was clear in the corridor, then dashed back to the stairs and hurried down to the ground floor. It was deserted.

They both realised that they were running out of time: at any moment Matheson would discover their escape. They ran for the door, not worrying about noise.

Outside, in the driveway, Grant's Jaguar was parked neatly on the gravel.

'She took my car!' exclaimed Grant, staring at it incredulously.

'More to the point,' said Rachel, 'can we take your car? Do you have your keys?'

Grant shook his head. 'I left them in my desk; Olivia must have taken them. But there's a spare under the chassis. Let's go!'

He pelted across the gravel to the Jaguar with Rachel in hot pursuit, then dropped to the ground and slid head and shoulders under the car.

Minute followed heart-stopping minute. She could hear Grant muttering numbers under his breath. A spare key on a bit of string or tape hadn't been good enough for the Jag, for obvious reasons; no, it had a marvel of a combination-locked box which not only kept out thieves but was an effective owner-deterrent as well. Grant had moved on from numbers to more interesting language; Rachel had stopped breathing. Why didn't he *hurry*?

At last, when her heart seemed to have lodged permanently in her throat, he rolled out from under the car with a shout of triumph and leapt to his feet. He unlocked his own door, dropped into the seat, and unlocked Rachel's door in the same instant that he turned on the ignition.

The door of the house opened behind them.

Rachel ran round to the passenger side, got in, and slammed the door. The Jaguar took off in a hail of gravel.

As they pulled away from the house, Rachel heard odd pinging sounds from the back of the car. She thought at first it was gravel flying up; then there was a loud cracking noise from the rear window.

Rachel turned around in her seat. There was, she discovered, an unmistakable bullet hole in the rear window of the car.

So much had happened that she couldn't even feel afraid. At least Grant would be happy, she thought resignedly. Someone was shooting at him at last.

'The nerve of these people,' said Grant, gunning the accelerator. 'You don't shoot at a car like this; you might hurt it.'

'They might hurt us too,' Rachel pointed out.

'Not a hope,' said Grant. 'Their aim is atrocious. It was probably in much more danger just being driven by Olivia. If I'd realised she was the kind of girl to endanger an innocent car I'd have *known* I couldn't trust her—it just never occurred to me that anyone could sink so low.' The Jaguar was already half a mile from the house. Rachel realised that the shots had died down. Grant grinned at her. 'They can't have wanted to kill us, you know. Too dangerous. Probably just wanted to puncture a tyre.'

The car hurtled down another mile or so of driveway and out onto the main road.

'Now,' said Grant, in a tone of strong resolution, 'there's something I've got to do that can't wait any longer.'

'Call the police?' Rachel said hopefully.

'Oh, no, *that* can wait. Something much more important.' He gave the steering wheel a sudden spin; the car turned, on two wheels, into a narrow side road which twisted erratically into a wood. A couple of minutes went by, while they went deeper into the wood. At last he pulled the car off onto a grassy space and turned off the engine.

Rachel stared blankly around her.

'Rachel,' said Grant, turning to face her, 'there's something I've got to talk to you about.'

Suddenly Rachel understood. 'If you don't want to call the police after all, I'll understand,' she said hesitantly. 'I know how you must feel.'

'Do you, now?' His voice was odd.

'I heard what they were saying,' said Rachel. 'I recognised Olivia's voice. It must have been a terrible shock for you.'

Grant was staring at her, his expression as odd as his tone of voice. 'Rachel—'

'Why don't we just go back to my aunt's house?' she said. 'I'm sure I'll be right as rain in a day or so. Why, I feel better already,' she assured him. 'What's one little bump on the head and a couple of scraped wrists? I won't bother about pressing charges if you'd rather just forget the whole thing.'

Grant's eyes sparkled suddenly. 'Spoken like a real trooper,' he said. 'But that wasn't what I was thinking about. I don't know whether you realise it, but most of my money was tied up in the company.'

'Was it?' asked Rachel sympathetically.

'My shares are practically worthless now. Our rating shot through the roof when people recognised the potential of the wonder drug a couple of years ago—I grabbed the chance to issue more shares and raise capital for the conference centre and science park. I had to move fast because it was a good location and going for a great price. Now the stock market has overreacted—the value of the shares has fallen so far it'll take a miracle to get people interested again. It'll take money to fight Glomac, but the only way I could get it now would be to sell more shares—and right now Glomac are the only people in the market for them.'

'Hmm,' said Rachel. She couldn't see why Grant was bothering to tell her all this. He must know she didn't know anything about finance.

'I'm not a millionaire, Rachel. I'm broke, and probably out of a job, but I think I can consider myself released from my engagement. Will you marry me?'

'Of course,' said Rachel. 'But—'

She never got to finish the sentence. He pulled her into his arms and began kissing her with a thoroughness and enthusiasm that made all the other times look like practice runs.

Rachel put her arms round his neck and kissed him back. She knew she was probably insane. She'd just agreed to spend the rest of her life with a man who would probably spend the rest of *his* life alternately dodging and chasing desperadoes. Once, nothing would have seemed too high a price to pay to escape wading through swamps and hacking through jungles. Now, she realised recklessly, she simply didn't care where she went as long as Grant was there too.

His mouth lingered on hers with the heady sweetness she remembered. She'd never realised that you could be so happy it hurt: whenever she thought that he was actually hers she felt as though her heart might burst through her ribs. She could spend the rest of her life kissing Grant while the bullets whizzed overhead. She could do all the unthinkable things she'd kept thinking of when he'd belonged to somebody else. In fact, she realised, her mouth curling wickedly under his, she could hardly wait to get him somewhere really private.

'I think we both know that we'd be good together...' She remembered the grim frustration when he'd tried to put her out of his life. Well, they *would* be good together. They'd be wonderful together. It would be wonderful even when they weren't making love...

Rachel could remember trying to explain her feelings to Driscoll, his frequent complete inability to understand her. Grant, on the other hand, understood her almost without any need for words. She hadn't realised it was possible to be so happy.

He raised his head at last, the impossibly blue eyes holding her mesmerised. 'God, what a fool I've been!'

He bent his head again, his lips grazing hers. Rachel knew how he felt: it was hard to get used to the idea that each kiss was not the last, that there was absolutely no reason not to have another. It was hard to get used to not having to watch herself all the time, to not worrying about whether she was going too far. Well, maybe not that hard, she decided, burying her hands in his hair. She coaxed his mouth open again, her lips soft against his, then thrust her tongue deep inside. He laughed deep in his throat, his arms tightening around her again.

This time it was Rachel who at last, reluctantly, broke free. 'This is ridiculous, Grant,' she said, forcing herself not to kiss the firm sensuous mouth again. 'We should be doing something practical. We've got the rest of our lives for this kind of thing.'

'Well, you know what they say,' said Grant. 'Today is the first day of the rest of your life. Always begin as you mean to go on. Pleasure before duty—that's my motto.'

Rachel laughed. 'Well, you're the ex-multimillionaire,'

she said. 'If you're not worried about it, who am I to complain?'

He grinned. 'I don't know, you might have a hankering after Paris couture. Sure you don't mind?'

'Is that a serious question?'

'Semi-serious. I didn't give you much time to think just now.'

Rachel scowled at him. 'I don't think of marriage as a strategy for updating my wardrobe,' she informed him. 'That's the stupidest thing I've ever heard.'

He shrugged. 'Well, it mattered to Olivia.'

'I'm not Olivia,' snapped Rachel.

The blue eyes lit with amusement. 'I know you're not, R. K. V. It's one of the things I like best about you.' He ran a careless finger through the black thatch of hair; a tingle of electricity ran up her spine. 'Never mind, Spidergirl. If we scrimp and save maybe I'll be able to buy you a new spidersuit for our golden wedding.'

'You may be out of a job,' retorted Rachel, 'but I'm a highly sought-after environmental impact assessor. If you're nice maybe I'll buy you a new tie once in a while.'

'Now that I'm an ex-businessman I don't have to wear a tie,' he protested. 'But if you promise not to buy me any I'll be as nice as I know how.' He bent his head and brushed her lips again with a feather-light kiss.

Rachel laughed and shook her head, responding more to the glowing look in his eyes than to the words. She felt as though she'd never really appreciated him before.

Rachel had been through so many crises with Driscoll that she knew every form the bruised male ego could take when it had had a battering. Sometimes she'd felt as if she'd developed a kind of sixth sense for the wounded self-esteem that could lurk under even an appearance of jauntiness. Now, though, the sixth sense found nothing to work on. If Grant had been putting a good front on bitter disappointment and resentment, she would have known—but he wasn't.

He was as genuinely exuberant and light-hearted as he'd been the day they'd first met, when the world had been at his feet. In some men, that might have been a sign of irresponsibility, of an inability to face the facts. With Grant, though, it seemed to be proof of an absolutely unshakeable self-confidence. Driscoll, who'd had no self-confidence, had had to insist that everything he did was right. Grant, she suspected, would be the first to admit that he had made a few mistakes which had contributed to the present setback. The reason was that he simply wouldn't care.

Grant, she thought, would fight to get back what was his, and would probably get it; it was hard for Rachel to believe that he could fail to get something if he put his mind to it. If he didn't, though, he would move on to something else and make a success of that instead. That conviction of being able to make his way in the world would always be with him. For all his joking, easygoing manner, he had an inner strength which far surpassed anything she'd ever come across.

'You know, I'm almost glad this has happened,' she said, feeling as always that she could tell him whatever she thought. 'It's easy to underestimate you. After all, lots of people can be laid back when they have money to cushion them. It's when things go wrong that they fall apart.'

She smiled at him rather shyly. 'Whereas you really don't mind! I don't think I could have believed that if I hadn't seen it with my own eyes. I've never met anyone like you. You shrug off things that would devastate other people.'

For once he seemed at a loss for words. His hand traced the line of her jaw while he searched for an answer. At last he said ruefully, 'I think you're giving me too much credit, Rachel. The last few months have been absolute hell: knowing I couldn't have you, trying to pretend I didn't care. I may not have fallen apart, but I did the next worst thing, throwing myself into a kind of senseless workaholism, trying to work so hard I couldn't think.'

He grinned wryly. 'Well, I certainly succeeded there. I managed to blind myself to some really fundamental problems until the whole thing blew up in my face.'

'But you're not worried about it,' said Rachel. 'You're not sitting here trying to tell me you're the businessman of the century even though you just happened to lose your company through a small oversight.'

'In other words, my ego is so colossal I don't need you to bolster it,' he said cheerfully. 'I love it when you love me for my faults. Seriously, though, I may have lost a lot of money, but I can always get more—and at least I don't have to feel guilty about Olivia. She was working so hard to make a success of the project that I felt trapped; I couldn't even think of letting her down when she'd been so loyal. The way I feel now, escape is cheap at the price. Would you marry Driscoll for the sake of a few million? The hell you would.'

Rachel gave up the struggle. It made a change to have a man do something really extraordinary and insist that it was nothing to make a fuss about. Somehow she thought she could get used to it.

'All right, you win,' she said. 'The money is nothing. But the science park is your baby. You can't give that up without a fight. Isn't there anything we can do? Can't the police do anything?'

'"Constable, my ex-fiancée hired the ex-fiancé of my fiancée to identify a common sparrow as a Savi's Warbler. I demand that you arrest her instantly." I'm sure they'd find it very entertaining.'

'We were kidnapped,' Rachel protested. '*That's* not a joke.'

'Of course not, but the question is how to get my company back on track,' he pointed out. 'Ever head of a poison pill?'

'The kind of thing spies have?'

'Or companies. It's a safeguard against takeovers,' he explained. 'You have a lot of clauses written into your constitution that make it hard for someone else to make a quick profit if they buy you out. Mine includes a lot of things that require approval of seventy-five per cent of the shareholders—in particular, radical changes in dealings with my old pals in the Amazon, since the drug I told you about was one of the things likeliest to attract an outsider. I've only got thirty per cent of the shares, but it's enough to block anything I don't like. On the other hand, obviously they can buy up enough to block anything I might want to do.'

'But why would Glomac try this if it wasn't going to do them any good?' asked Rachel.

Grant shrugged. 'In the first place, they were obviously in a hurry: they had to move as soon as the share prices dropped. They couldn't afford to wait, in case I managed to kill the story. That seems to have happened by accident—it looks as though I have Driscoll to thank for that. In the second place, it's obvious Olivia thought she could talk me round. She probably persuaded Matheson that she could deliver the goods.'

'But once they know she can't, won't they just back down?'

'More likely try to starve me out,' he said cynically.

'But if you could kill the story now, share prices would go back up, wouldn't they?' asked Rachel. 'So they'd make a profit if they sold, and they'd have no reason to keep them if they couldn't use the company the way they wanted.'

'It's a possibility,' he agreed. 'But it's not an easy story to kill. We can go back and get soil samples again from the plants, and maybe prove that that was a set-up. A bird is something else again. How do you prove that someone didn't see a bird he said he did?'

'So we need a confession,' Rachel said despondently.

'Looks that way. How do you fancy your chances with Driscoll?'

'Not good,' she admitted. 'What about Olivia?'

'What do you think?' He grimaced.

There was a gloomy silence. At last Grant shrugged. 'Rachel, I'm not saying it looks hopeful, but in my experience you tend to find inspiration unexpectedly when you're in a tight corner. You're better off trying to come up with an unorthodox solution that looks as though it might work than wasting energy on obvious things that seem pointless but are easy to do.'

'But—' Rachel began.

'Look, I may not think much of my chances of getting Olivia to come clean, but they'll be roughly nil if I introduce her to the pleasure of a police cell. Let's not do things just for the sake of doing *something*.'

'So you think we should just sit here and do nothing?' Rachel asked impatiently.

'I didn't say that,' he protested. 'I thought we were making the best possible use of our time, before you interrupted and started going on about the police.'

Rachel laughed. 'All right, I take back the nothing. I agree that kissing me is an unorthodox solution to the problem. My only question is, what makes you think it might work?'

'There speaks the typical scientist. Sceptical to the core.' His mouth quirked up in amusement. 'Let's just say that, in my experience, inspiration never comes when you look for it. The best plan is to think about something else and see what happens. Does that satisfy your conscience, Dr Hawkins?'

'Of course,' said Rachel promptly. 'And, just out of scientific interest, would you say that kissing someone was the most effective way of not looking for inspiration?'

'I never answer leading questions,' he murmured. He bent his head and kissed her lightly. Rachel took a sharp breath. 'I think I can say, though,' he said very softly, his mouth only a breath away from hers, 'that kissing you beats any other way of not looking for inspiration that I've ever come across.'

His mouth took possession of hers. Rachel gave up the argument. Why had she thought he was being impractical? He was simply not looking for inspiration in the most distracting, most effective way possible. She should have known.

CHAPTER FIFTEEN

IN THE end it was frustration rather than inspiration that stopped them: the gear lever, the steering wheel and the bucket seats kept jabbing them. At last Grant leant back against his seat and glared out of the window.

'Are you thinking what I'm thinking?' he asked, his voice rough.

'I don't know,' Rachel said hoarsely, trying to control her breathing. 'I'm thinking that I'm staying with my aunt and uncle, who would probably put us in a room with twin beds even if we were *married*, that you own a house with fifty bedrooms that's in the hands of your ex-fiancée-if-she-only-knew-it; and that your money and credit cards are probably in a wallet in a jacket which I notice you're not wearing. Is that what you were thinking?'

'More or less.' He rubbed his hand over his jaw and grimaced. 'And also that I need a shave.'

'We'd better go to my aunt's house,' Rachel said reluctantly. 'At least we can get something to eat. I'm *so* hungry.'

He agreed to this and turned on the ignition. The car made a tight circle, then headed back to the main road.

There was no sign of their enemies. 'Since we took this car, they'll be bound to realise I'm back,' said Grant. 'That may be a good thing. It'll probably make them nervous; they may start to make mistakes.'

Rachel agreed to this doubtfully. As far as she could see, the situation was hopeless. She couldn't see what kind of

mistake their opponents could make that would do Grant
any good.

Aunt Harriet exclaimed in horror over the appearance of
the two battered arrivals on her doorstep. She allowed them
to go upstairs to wash and change, Rachel into clean
clothes, Grant into a dressing gown of Uncle Walter's. She
then watched with satisfaction while they wolfed down
most of the contents of the kitchen.

'Oh, Aunt Harriet,' said Rachel through a full mouth,
'congratulate me! We're engaged.'

'She's supposed to congratulate me,' Grant corrected her.
'You just get felicitations.'

'Well, I'm glad to hear it,' said Aunt Harriet. 'At least
now I'll get rid of that pesky tarantula. But I'm not sure if
I *can* congratulate you, Grant. Rachel always seems to get
into such a lot of trouble.'

'The better for me to get her out again,' he said cheerfully. 'And I like William. How is the little devil, anyway?'

'I really couldn't say,' Aunt Harriet replied stiffly. 'I'd
rather not think about him, and I find I can't help thinking
about him if I look at him, so I haven't been looking at
him.'

He grinned. 'Well, I can only say that you can't be more
anxious to find him a new home than I am to give him one.
The sooner I get Rachel under my own roof the better.'

Aunt Harriet suggested acerbically that he would be very
welcome to take the spider *before* the wedding.

'I'm afraid Grant needs to stay here,' said Rachel, and
sketched in the situation.

'Ah,' said Aunt Harriet. 'Well, you can borrow a pair of
Walter's pyjamas tonight, Grant, and I'll try to clean those
things of yours for tomorrow. I don't suppose you'd care
to be seen in public in his ordinary clothes.'

Rachel suspected that, if the truth were known, Grant

would just as soon not take the pyjamas either, but he accepted the offer politely.

They spent the rest of the day eating, snatching kisses in corners when they could escape Aunt Harriet's eagle eye, and arguing about the best way to tackle Glomac.

Evening came without further inspiration. They went upstairs, and Aunt Harriet escorted Grant to a room at the opposite end of the corridor from Rachel's. A prim single bed, immaculately made up, stood against one wall.

'There you are,' said Aunt Harriet. 'Breakfast at eight o'clock.' She laid a clean pair of pyjamas on the bed, and stood with arms folded. Under that eagle eye Grant kissed Rachel chastely on the cheek.

'Good night, Spidergirl. Pleasant dreams.' His eyes gleamed.

Rachel went to her room and slipped into her own pyjamas. She heard Aunt Harriet stumping down the stairs, presumably to wash out Grant's clothes.

About ten minutes later there was a soft knock at the door. It opened and Grant strolled in.

Rachel stifled a laugh behind her hand. Uncle Walter's pyjama bottoms stopped about halfway down Grant's calves. An ample waist was now gathered in copious folds by the cord now tied around the narrow hips of the wearer while, below, the cotton strained over muscular thighs. He'd buttoned one button of the top, which closed easily over a lean belly and gaped suddenly across a broad, powerful chest.

'Oh, dear,' Rachel said faintly. 'I'm afraid they don't fit terribly well,' she sputtered. 'What are you doing here, anyway?'

'I've come to say goodnight to William,' he explained. He approached the glass case and peered solemnly down. William crouched motionless in a corner.

'He's sleeping,' said Grant. 'I won't wake him.'

Rachel choked down a laugh.

'But since I'm here it seems a shame to waste a golden opportunity,' he remarked. He came and sat beside her on the bed, the pyjama bottoms straining at the seams.

'I don't like to be a wet blanket,' said Rachel, 'but I think Aunt Harriet was trying to give you a hint by putting you in that bedroom.'

'It would take more than a hint and a pair of tight pyjamas to keep me away from you,' he said, grinning and putting an arm around her. 'She could try chaining me to the bedpost...'

'Well, you'd probably pick the lock with your teeth,' said Rachel. She raised a hand to his silky smooth cheek. 'Mmm, lovely.'

He kissed her hungrily. No wonder, she thought; it had been nearly two hours. Rachel struggled briefly with temptation and gave in; she unbuttoned the button of his pyjama top and slid her hand round to the hard, muscular back.

He groaned deep in his throat and fell back on the bed, drawing her with him and pulling her hard up against him. Rachel tried to relax. She wished she could enjoy this. Well, she was enjoying it, but she actually felt more nervous now, when the most dangerous thing that could come through the door was her aunt with a glass of hot milk, than she had in their attic prison when armed desperadoes might have burst into the room.

'Grant,' she murmured, 'what if my aunt comes in?'

'I've got one foot on the floor,' he said, lifting his head for a moment. She could feel his warm breath against her mouth. 'If it's good enough for the old Hollywood censors it should be good enough for your aunt.'

The blue eyes were limpid with innocence.

'I don't know about my aunt,' said Rachel, 'but, considering what you can do with your feet bound and both hands tied behind your back, it would take a lot more than one foot on the floor to set *my* mind at rest.'

She let her head fall back on the pillow and looked up

into his face, running her fingers through the thick blond hair. 'Isn't there any way you can get those people out of Arrowmead?' she asked huskily. 'I want to cast aside my inhibitions.'

'I suppose it'll have to be that,' he said. 'I can hardly just take you along to the wedding and say I've found a better bride.' He ran his hand lightly along the line of her hip.

'Actually, I think it might help if I just talked to Olivia,' he added thoughtfully. 'She has a lot of debts. I think she must have got nervous when I explained that what I had in mind wasn't likely to show a profit for a long time. Glomac must have looked a better bet, but she's obviously got into something a lot nastier than she expected. Maybe I could offer her some kind of deal to get her out of a tight spot...'

Rachel refrained from comment. If all Grant's hunches had been as brilliant as this idea of appealing to Olivia's better nature, something told her, he'd have had an over-draft the size of the national debt. With any luck he'd have a better idea if she didn't say anything.

'I just don't see—I mean, do you think she was really planning to marry you?' she asked instead. It was wonderful to have him actually in her arms while she asked this, wonderful to have solid proof that he was indisputably hers.

'Looks that way.' He smiled, tugging one of her soot-black locks of hair. 'I suppose she thought I'd be better off financially in the long run. That was all that *really* mattered to her, so she probably thought the end justified the means for me too, that I just didn't know where my own interest lay.

'Anyway, if she tells Matheson she'll confess, he'll have to back down to keep his nose clean.'

'I hope you're right,' said Rachel. 'Just be careful, will you? Sort it out over the phone, or in writing, or something. You've robbed these people of the chance to shoot at your tyres, you know. They may aim at your head in sheer frustration.'

'Oh, sure,' said Grant. 'You know I never take risks.'

'Never *what*?'

'Unnecessary risks,' he amended. 'And, speaking of frustration, maybe I'd better go back to my room. Maybe I'll strike it lucky and dream about you.'

'I thought I was always out of reach in your dreams,' said Rachel.

'Yes, but that was before you knew my intentions were honourable. Now that we're engaged you may stop playing hard to get.' He sat up reluctantly, refastening the single button. 'I'll let you know at breakfast how we get on.'

'If you don't respect me in the morning I'll know why,' said Rachel.

'You know I'll always respect you, R. K. V.,' he said seriously. 'It's an odd experience to respect someone who drives you mad with lust, but if you ask me it's the basis for a perfect marriage.' He flicked her chin with a finger. 'Sweet dreams, darling.'

'You said that before,' said Rachel.

'Well, don't do anything I wouldn't do.' He grinned and disappeared through the door.

Rachel slept badly. Her dreams were fitful and sinister. They were not, as she'd rather hoped, of Grant in his ill-fitting pyjamas, of herself removing the ill-fitting pyjamas and falling into his arms. Instead she dreamt of faceless, ominous enemies who closed in on Grant. She saw him going forward to meet someone as a friend, then falling to the ground in an ambush, and each time she could do nothing to stop it. Each time she was too late.

It was a relief to wake up. It was only a dream, she reminded herself. She'd see him at breakfast, and then refuse to let him out of her sight. It was as simple as that.

The sight of him at breakfast, in his own clothes, was reassuring.

'Pleasant dreams?' she asked, helping herself to toast.

'I never kiss and tell,' he said with a grin. 'I've got a couple of phone calls to make, then we'll go into town. I need to see a solicitor.'

He disappeared into Uncle Walter's office to make the necessary phone calls. By ten he and Rachel were back in the Jaguar, bowling into town.

'Did you talk to Olivia?' she asked. 'What did she say?'

'Well, all is not lost, but it'll take some unravelling. Too complicated to go into now.'

They got into town too early for the appointment with Uncle Walter's solicitor, and wandered about window-shopping. Grant insisted on going into a toy-shop and buying Rachel a large black plastic tarantula.

'A memento of the day we first met,' he said cheerfully.

Rachel pointed out a number of anatomical inaccuracies on the creature, then shrugged and laughed and thrust it into a pocket.

Grant then explained that his business with the solicitor might take some time.

'I asked some of my London staff to take the fast train down,' he went on. 'Your uncle's solicitor has kindly agreed to let me use a room. It may be a few hours. Can you amuse yourself in town? Then you can meet me back here—say around three?'

Rachel agreed to this, and they parted company at the solicitor's door.

After about half an hour she began to get bored. Her lunch hours at Murcheson's had left her all too familiar with the clothes in the shops, and she didn't share Olivia's passion for furniture. At last she bought a book on wildlife in the African veld and headed back for the solicitor's. She'd read in the waiting room, she decided.

The secretary greeted her politely. 'Can I help you?' she asked.

'I thought I'd just sit here and read while Mr Mallett has his meeting,' said Rachel. 'I understand he's using one of your rooms.'

'Oh, no,' said the girl. 'Mr Mallett left ten minutes ago.' She smiled. 'We're a very small office, you know. We don't have a spare room that could be used for a meeting.'

'I see,' said Rachel. She left without further argument, her book still in her hand. He'd *lied* to her. But why?

With a sinking heart, she realised that she knew very well why. Why do things the safe way, when he could go and offer a bunch of thugs a little extra target practice? Mr Grant 'No Unnecessary Risks' Mallett was heading for Arrowmead at this very minute, or she'd eat her hat.

She looked for the Jaguar just to give him the benefit of the doubt, but wasn't surprised that it was gone.

'I'll *kill* him!' she growled to herself. She just hoped nobody else got to him first, because she was going to tear him limb from limb.

She would tear him limb from limb in private, after it was all over. Meanwhile she'd had enough of amateur heroics. It was time to call in the police.

Rachel ran breathlessly up the cobbled high street to the police station and encountered an unexpected setback. The station was only manned part-time: its hours were posted outside, and it was already closed for the day. A number was given for emergencies.

Rachel ran back down the high street to the single public telephone. It was out of order.

All right, so it was out of order. There was no need to panic, she told herself. Panicking, she ran even more breathlessly to Joyce's antique shop.

'I've got to call the police!' she panted. 'Can't explain!'
There was no reply when she called the emergency num-

ber. She tried numbers for several of the surrounding villages with no better success.

So much for calling in the experts.

Rachel poured out her dilemma to her old friend. Ten minutes later she was bounding over the road to Arrowmead in Joyce's van.

Rachel didn't like the idea of going back and facing people who'd hit her over the head and tied her up, and who might decide, this time, to put her out of commission permanently. The problem was that she liked the idea of Grant's facing these people alone even less. Mouth set grimly, she gunned the accelerator, and was soon twisting along the drive to Arrowmead.

She stopped the van out of sight of the house, and pulled it off the road to park it behind a thick stand of rhododendron. Then she gritted her teeth and set off for the house.

No one seemed to be about, but a curtain was billowing out of one of the windows of Grant's office. If the window was open, maybe that meant someone was in.

Rachel entered the house unchallenged, heart thumping in her chest.

Moving as silently as she could, she crept along the magnificent corridors of the ground floor to the wing which held Grant's office.

The secretary's office was empty. Voices were coming faintly from Grant's office through the closed door. Rachel tried it very carefully. It was locked.

She hesitated, then bent to listen at the keyhole.

'Now what do we do?' It was a man's voice—one she didn't recognise.

'I'm not sure.' The cool, certain voice didn't match the words. 'We may have gone too far to go back.'

'You mean...?'

'We've got to consider the possibility. He's made a will in my favour, you know.' There was a short pause. 'It might be simpler if everything were under my control.'

'We'd better decide one way or the other. He'll be coming round soon. He's got a head like a rock. Shall I tie him up again?'

'Don't you think the two of us can deal with him?' Olivia sneered. 'He's not Superman, you know.'

'All right, whatever you say. So what shall we do?'

Rachel didn't stop to hear more. One thing was clear: there was no time to call in the police. Any minute now Olivia might decide to be a wealthy widow without bothering with the wedding.

What could she do, though? Shout through the door that Grant had made another will? Preposterous. Bang on the door, then hit them over the head when they came to investigate? Absurd.

No, she thought, but if she could somehow buy more time...

Suddenly her eyes fell upon the phone. It had five or six lines; it would be simple enough to call Grant's personal number on one of the other lines. It was risky, of course, because both lines would light up on Grant's phone; if Olivia stopped to think, she would realise that the call was coming from inside the building. Still, it was worth a try.

She tiptoed across the room, picked up the receiver and dialled Grant's direct line. The phone rang, and rang, and rang. Was Olivia going to leave it to ring? she wondered in despair. On the eighth ring, however, the receiver was lifted at the other end.

'Arrowmead Conference Centre,' Olivia said curtly.

'May I speak to Mr Mallett? I'm calling from the solicitor's office,' said Rachel, disguising her voice with a nasal falsetto.

'I'm afraid he's stepped out of the office,' Olivia said smoothly. 'I'll be happy to take a message.'

'We just have a question about the will he had Mr Fairfax draw up this morning,' said Rachel. 'He said we could send the invoice to the office, but he asked us to send the actual document to the residence of a Rachel Hawkins. It seemed rather irregular; we just wanted to make sure there was no mistake.'

'Oh, I rather think there *has* been a mistake,' said Olivia, with scarcely a pause. 'Please send both the invoice and the will to the office.'

Rachel scowled. Clever Olivia! She'd obviously seen her way at once to destroying the will.

'I'm afraid I need to confirm that with Mr Mallett personally,' Rachel said pompously. 'Perhaps you could give him the message.'

'I can assure you I speak for Mr Mallett,' Olivia said sharply. 'I'm—I'm his personal private secretary. He will find it extremely inconvenient if the will isn't sent to his office.'

'We shall be happy to send it to the office,' Rachel said starchily, 'as soon as we receive authorisation to that effect from Mr Mallett. Kindly ask him to call us at his earliest convenience.' She hung up the phone.

Well, she reflected, that should at least give Olivia pause for thought. It still left Grant unconscious, though, and unable to defend himself.

Her eyes narrowed. Grant's office looked out, she remembered, onto a sunken garden. Latticed trellises climbed the walls, framing French windows onto tiny individual balconies. It was true, of course, that roses climbed the trellises, so that ascending them would be a delicate business. Still, it was not impossible, she decided.

That wouldn't help, she knew, if she couldn't get in that way either. She remembered the curtain whipping in the wind, though; wasn't it possible that with so much else going on that open window might have been overlooked? She could at least go out and see.

If it was, it would take her some time to get in. By that time, Grant might be conscious, and between the two of them they might do something.

There were an awful lot of possibles and mights to this scenario, but it made her nervous to think of Grant at the mercy of those two. Olivia was still just about rational, but she was in a tight spot. At any minute she might lose her nerve. If she had a gun, it might not take too much to make it go off in Grant's direction, will or no will.

Ten minutes later Rachel stood looking up at Grant's office from the ground. The air was still, but she could see that the window was still open. Wonderful, she thought sourly. So now all she had to do was climb up through this blasted rose-bush and come to the rescue.

Without the rose-bush, the climb might have taken a minute or two. Contending with the thorns, Rachel took a solid fifteen minutes. Each move involved moving a hand or foot to a new resting place, then prising free the briar that had fastened itself to sleeve or trouser leg. By the time she had reached the top she had decided not to tear Grant limb from limb after all. She would stick pins in him instead.

At last she stood on the tiny balcony. Inside, Olivia and her comrade were still arguing.

'At least let me tie him up,' said the man. 'Look, he's stirring now.'

'You've got a gun, for heaven's sake,' Olivia said contemptuously.

Rachel slipped behind the curtain and peeped into the room.

Grant sat on a chair, his hair matted with blood. He was staring dully ahead. As Rachel took in the scene, though, his gaze shifted slightly, and his eyes widened as he caught her eye.

Olivia sat at the desk, her back to Rachel. Rachel couldn't tell whether she had a gun or not. The man was leaning against the desk, holding a gun and looking rather uneasily at Grant.

Rachel looked again at Grant. What did he want her to

do? They would only have one chance, she thought grimly. Was he fit enough for a fight?

His face was very pale. Rachel forced herself to wait. There was no point in rushing things.

'I don't care what you say, I'm going to tie him up,' the man said sulkily. 'I saw some gaffer tape in the storeroom.'

'All right.' Olivia shrugged. 'Leave me the gun, then. I'll keep him covered.'

The man left the room. Olivia went round to the front of the desk and held the gun aimed at Grant.

His eyes were open now, though he was obviously having trouble sitting up. His mouth quirked in amusement at the gun. 'Second thoughts, darling?' he asked. 'Why didn't you say?'

Olivia made an impatient gesture with her gun hand. 'I'm sorry it had to come to this, Grant,' she said. 'Of course it's absurd. Why did you have to be such a bloody fool, though? You were sitting on a gold-mine. You could have named your price.'

'It's always such a tragedy, isn't it, when people don't like the same jokes?' said Grant. 'Here you thought you'd found a solvent man, GSOH—good sense of humour,' he translated helpfully. 'A lovely girl like you wouldn't go trawling the lonely hearts so you wouldn't know that. And then to find someone hell-bent on destroying his liquidity, *and* with no sense of humour worth speaking of!'

'Oh, you were always very amusing,' said Olivia.

'But not amused, darling,' he said drily. 'Not at all amused by the way you had Rachel attacked.'

'That little meddler!' Olivia said viciously. 'I tried to get rid of her, but would she listen? No! She had to poke her nose in. Well, it served her right. I hope it taught her a lesson!'

This, Rachel decided, was her cue.

'Olivia!' she called.

Olivia whipped round.

Rachel stepped through the curtains. 'Look out!' she shouted. And she hurled something large and black and leggy at the other woman.

Olivia recoiled instinctively.

The split second was all Grant needed. He hurled himself forward, knocking the gun to the ground.

Olivia screamed. Footsteps thundered down the corridor outside. Grant snatched up the gun; in two strides he had reached the door and placed himself just inside.

Griffiths burst through the door and was knocked to the ground as Grant brought the gun down on the back of his neck.

But now, from further away, they heard voices and more running footsteps.

Grant's eyes swept the room, and came to rest on the walk-in closet.

'Well, much as I hate to leave you this way...' he murmured to Olivia. Her eyes moved nervously from Grant to the unconscious figure on the floor. Before she realised what he had in mind, Grant took her by the shoulders and bundled her into the closet. He slammed the door shut, then locked the door to the office and began blockading it with furniture.

Rachel spotted the roll of gaffer tape on the ground beside Griffiths. She snatched it up and rolled it around his arms several times.

Grant glanced down. 'Well done, Spidergirl!' He grinned. 'Now, let's get out of here.'

He strode across the room to a window and threw it open. It was around the corner from the one Rachel had entered, and though it had a trellis the gardeners hadn't yet persuaded roses to climb up it.

'Ladies first,' he said, with a bow and a flourish. Fists were pounding on the door behind them. Rachel swarmed down the trellis, closely followed by Grant.

They took off across the lawn. Grant seemed to run effortlessly, in spite of his ordeal; Rachel had trouble keeping up. At last the driveway was in sight. She put on a burst of speed. Suddenly there was a searing pain in her arm— and for the second time that week everything went black.

Rachel came to in the front seat of the Jaguar. Grant was driving it along the road to the village with more than his usual urgency; his profile was grim. She thought for a moment of asking what had happened, caught a glimpse of the speedometer and thought again. Her arm was throbbing; after a minute or so she fell into an uneasy half-sleep.

About ten minutes went by; Grant was negotiating the streets of the town. The car bounced over the cobbles, took a turn, and slowed abruptly. Grant swore under his breath as the Jaguar drifted implacably to a halt.

The next thing she knew, Rachel was being carried in Grant's arms through the streets. The movement jarred her arm painfully; she drifted in and out of consciousness, and woke at last in her aunt's living room.

She was lying on the sofa, wrapped in a brightly coloured blanket. A fire was burning in the fireplace. There were low voices in the background.

'She'll be all right, Grant,' said Uncle Walter. 'It's just a flesh wound.' *Just*, thought Rachel indignantly. 'Why, a little thing like this is nothing to Rachel.'

'I did think she'd settle down like ordinary people with Driscoll,' said Aunt Harriet. 'But I suppose it's just in the blood.'

'She looks very pale,' Grant said anxiously. 'Shouldn't she see a doctor? I know you sterilised the wound but I still think an expert opinion wouldn't be amiss.'

'Never you mind,' Aunt Harriet said comfortably. 'She'll come round. Did she ever show you her scrapbook?'

'No.'

There was a brief pause while Aunt Harriet rooted about for this treasure.

'Look at this. SCHOOLGIRL EXPOSES TROPICAL BIRD RACKET. That was when she went on a school trip to the Amazon.' There was a rustling of pages. 'Or this one: BRITISH TOURIST UNCOVERS WHITE SLAVE TRADE. That was when she went on a package tour to Sicily with a couple of girlfriends.'

'Her leg was in a cast for weeks afterward, but that didn't faze Rachel one bit,' Uncle Walter said cheerfully.

Oh, *didn't* it? thought Rachel furiously.

'This is amazing,' said Grant. 'I always thought of R. K. V. Hawkins as a hardworking scientist who stayed out of trouble.'

'Oh, good heavens, no,' said Aunt Harriet. 'Whatever gave you that idea?'

'Well, she never said anything about it.'

'I wonder why?' speculated Uncle Walter.

'And these are all in Spanish,' continued Aunt Harriet. 'Don't ask me what it was all about, because I couldn't tell you, but I do know she made some depositions. Took a while for the black eye to fade, of course, but, after all, you can do so much with make-up.'

'Grant,' said Rachel faintly.

'Rachel!' He came instantly to her side. 'Are you all right? How do you feel?'

'Terrible,' she said bluntly. 'If you have to go on about that stuff, go into another room.'

'I told you she'd be all right,' Uncle Walter said cheerfully.

'We'll leave the two of you alone for now, Grant,' said Aunt Harriet. 'I'll just make sure your bed is ready in the spare room.'

'Thanks very much,' said Grant, sinking to one knee beside the sofa. At least he wasn't treating her like a rubber ball that always bounced back, thought Rachel. Grant hardly noticed when her aunt and uncle left the room: he was staring anxiously down into her face.

'What happened to your hands?' he asked. 'They're covered with scratches.'

'I climbed up that blasted rose trellis,' said Rachel.

'My poor Rachel,' he said. 'What a lot of trouble I've caused you.' He kissed her hands, then held them to his cheek.

Then, abruptly, he did a double take. 'The spare room,' he said. 'Did your aunt say something about the spare room?'

'Where you spent last night,' Rachel reminded him.

'Oh, yes, how kind,' said Grant. 'But I couldn't possibly settle in without making sure you'd had proper medical attention. It's the least I can do after all you've been through. Can you stand?'

'I think so, but it's really not necessary...' Rachel was beginning to feel guilty about having made such a fuss.

'Not another word,' said Grant. 'I'll get your uncle to lend me his car.' He scooped Rachel into his arms and strode for the door, where he nearly ran into Aunt Harriet bearing a clean towel.

'Rachel is feeling very strange,' he said to the astonished aunt. 'I'm taking her in just to be on the safe side.'

Half an hour later a doctor had confirmed that the wound needed no stitches and was clean. Grant ushered Rachel out to the car again. Fifteen minutes later it drew up in front of Arrowmead.

No bullets cracked the windscreen. No thugs ran across the lawn.

'Haven't you had enough for one day?' asked Rachel.

'They're all gone,' said Grant. 'In police custody. They've even picked up Matheson. I wanted to talk to Olivia alone, but I gave the police a time to show up half an hour after the time I'd set for my appointment just in case something went wrong. You know I never take unnecessary risks.'

'Well, I've often heard you say so,' Rachel said drily,

sparing a thought for all those unmanned police stations. 'Why did you go off without telling me?' she demanded accusingly.

'I didn't want you to get in any danger,' he explained. 'I thought you didn't like adventures.'

'I don't like adventures,' said Rachel. 'I hate being shot at. I hate being hit over the head. I hate broken bones. But if you ever go off without me again I'll tear you limb from limb.'

He smiled at her, and even though she was furious she found herself smiling helplessly back. 'This was a false start,' said Grant. 'Nothing like this will ever happen again.'

'All right,' said Rachel. That was one good thing about Grant: he was such an optimist. She raised one hand to his hair and stroked it.

'I had a voice-activated tape recorder attached to my body; I got a terrific confession from Olivia,' he explained eagerly. 'We'll get the science park back on track and settle down.'

'Mmm-hmm,' said Rachel.

'No one will ever shoot at you again,' he assured her. He looked rather the worse for wear himself: there was a bandage across his forehead, and an ugly bruise on one cheekbone. Rachel tried to imagine him leading a respectable life as one of the world's bystanders, and failed.

'Mmm-hmm,' said Rachel again.

He grinned. 'Well, if they do I promise I'll always be there to remind you to wear your bulletproof vest.'

Rachel tried unsuccessfully to frown. A little smile was tugging at the corner of her mouth. Maybe she'd been trying to change the wrong things. She'd tried to give up science altogether instead of finding a way of doing the science she liked. She'd tried to become the kind of person who turned a blind eye to trouble.

Maybe, she thought, it was because everyone around her

had tried to turn her inclinations into a straitjacket. Driscoll had left her to get on with boring specialisation because that was 'Rachel's field'. Her aunt and uncle and everyone else she knew had just left her to get into scrapes and struggle out of them because that was what they thought Rachel was like—it would never have occurred to any of them to join her in attacking a flagrant abuse, or in facing danger.

Well, you couldn't say that of Grant, she reflected. His instincts were the same as hers; they'd be a real team. And if he was there, would she be able to help having a wonderful time? No, Rachel realised wryly, she probably wouldn't. She could probably spend the next fifty years taking 'no unnecessary risks' with Grant and have the time of her life.

'Do you promise always to kiss it better if people beat me to a pulp?' she asked.

'Rachel, darling,' he protested, 'no one is going to beat you to a pulp. You're not listening to me. We're going to be respectable, law-abiding citizens doing business with other respectable, law-abiding citizens. We're going to settle down.' The brilliant blue eyes deepened from aquamarine to sapphire. 'But I promise to kiss you for strictly non-medicinal purposes on an extremely regular basis.'

He bent his head and kissed her.

'I hope you're not having second thoughts,' he added, raising his head and looking at her anxiously. 'I couldn't face another lonely night in your aunt's spare room, so I brought you back here instead.' He smiled at her. 'I just thought as long as we'd got rid of the household pests we needn't—er—impose on your aunt's hospitality any longer. Do you mind? I'll take you back if you want to go home.'

Some people, thought Rachel, might think it a bit of an imposition to take her uncle's car, leaving him the use of a Jaguar with an empty tank. She would have to point that out to Grant—some other time.

'You mean we're actually alone with a house with a double bed?' she asked.

'More like fifty last time I counted,' said Grant.

'Hmm,' said Rachel. There was really no point in arguing with Grant, who sincerely believed that he'd come to the end of his adventures. It would really be much better, on the whole, just to keep him occupied and make sure he kept out of trouble.

'Why don't we find one?' she said. 'I think we could both do with a good night's sleep.'

'Is that a polite way of saying a bad night's sleep?' asked Grant.

'What do you think?' countered Rachel.

'I think it means you don't want to go,' he said.

'No, I think I'll stay here,' said Rachel. 'You're absolutely right, Grant. It's time we settled down.'

HARLEQUIN PRESENTS

HARLEQUIN PRESENTS
men you won't be able to resist
falling in love with...

HARLEQUIN PRESENTS
women who have feelings
just like your own...

HARLEQUIN PRESENTS
powerful passion in
exotic international settings...

HARLEQUIN PRESENTS
intense, dramatic stories that will keep you
turning to the very last page...

HARLEQUIN PRESENTS
The world's bestselling romance series!

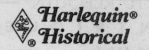

Harlequin® Historical

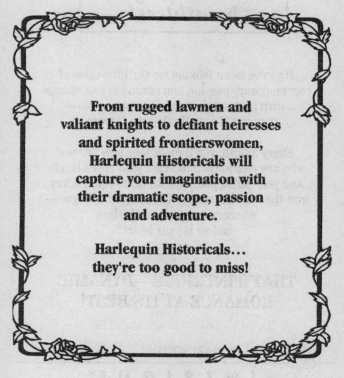

From rugged lawmen and
valiant knights to defiant heiresses
and spirited frontierswomen,
Harlequin Historicals will
capture your imagination with
their dramatic scope, passion
and adventure.

Harlequin Historicals…
they're too good to miss!

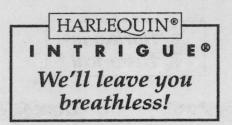

LOOK FOR OUR FOUR FABULOUS MEN!

Each month some of today's bestselling authors bring
four new fabulous men to Harlequin American Romance.
Whether they're rebel ranchers, millionaire power brokers
or sexy single dads, they're all gallant princes—and
they're all ready to sweep you into lighthearted fantasies
and contemporary fairy tales where anything is possible—
and where all your dreams come true!

You don't even have to make a wish…
Harlequin American Romance will grant your every desire!

Look for Harlequin American Romance
wherever Harlequin books are sold!

S HARLEQUIN SUPERROMANCE®

...there's more to the story!

Superromance. A *big* satisfying read about unforget-
table characters. Each month we offer
four very different stories that range from family
drama to adventure and mystery, from highly emotional stories to romantic comedies—and
much more! Stories about people you'll
believe in and care about. Stories too
compelling to put down....

Our authors are among today's *best* romance writ-
ers. You'll find familiar names and
talented newcomers. Many of them are
award winners—and you'll see why!

If you want the biggest and best
in romance fiction, you'll get it
from Superromance!

Available wherever Harlequin books are sold.

Look us up on-line at: http://www.romance.net

HS-GEN